Single Omega Dad

The Omega Misfits, Book 4

by

Wendy Rathbone

Single Omega Dad: The Omega Misfits Book 4
Copyright © June 2020 by Wendy Rathbone and Eye Scry
Publications.

A publication by: Eye Scry Publications
http://www.eyescrypublications.com

ISBN: 978-1-942415-35-0
TITLE: Single Omega Dad: The Omega Misfits Book 4
Author: Wendy Rathbone
Cover by: Wendy Rathbone

Address all inquiries to the author at:
wrathbone@juno.com

For Della, as always...

Acknowledgements

Special thanks to my beta readers:

Jackie North
Sera Trevor

Additional thanks to some wonderful readers who helped me come up with names for some of my characters.

Candice Clark Daley for Saber
Ulrika Lund for Volmar (Saber's last name)
Rosalind Stirzaker for Luke
Avril Marie for Mathias
Jeanette Cooper for Trigg

Single Omega Dad

Chapter One

Mathias

"My name is Chichi," said the Omega.

Obnoxiously cute, and I didn't care. I was hard and burning. He drew me into his embrace as if caught by my charm. But I didn't have charm when I was in the Burn. I saved that for my Alpha family or friends I wanted to like me. I didn't care if this Chichi liked me.

He didn't seem to care, either. He was pulled to me by his own hormones responding to my need. Already I could smell his arousal, like sugared strawberries, too strong for my tastes. In fact, it almost triggered my gag reflex. Awful. But my body surged, forcing me to take deep breaths of him, yearning to be surrounded by him.

Nausea and fucking were two things that did not go well together. But I didn't have a choice. I'd already chosen him out of the chattel catalog. I'd already paid.

Chichi had on the white shirt and black pants all the Zilly Farm whores wore. With a wide smile, he started to strip.

He had a lean waist, which I liked in my Omega rent boys, but he was too tall. I'd forgotten to look at all his details to check my preferences. But my cock throbbed anyway. My skin was flame.

Chichi, whose pale hair was shaved on one side so that it hung all to the left and over one eye, pushed his pants down to his ankles and stepped out of them, straightening to show me he was fully erect. He turned and presented himself to me, ass up, leaning down, his elbows on the red-draped, king-sized bed which was provided in all Zilly's mating rooms.

Towels lay next to the bed. Lube. Cock rings. Ball harnesses. Anal plugs. Everything we might need or want.

I liked cock rings and I already had one on. Silver. Extra large. I used it as an excuse for why I didn't knot. If asked about it, I would say, "I don't give my knot to any Omega. You have to earn it."

In truth, I couldn't knot. Never had. I'd suppressed my feelings of inadequacy about that for twelve years. No one knew except my brother Trigg. No one else would ever know, and honestly, I tried not to think about it much.

My orgasms during my Burns did not seem to be decreased by my inability to knot. Sometimes I felt relieved not to have prolonged body-locks with Omegas. To hear other Alphas talk about it, their partners would screech "Oh! Oh! Oh!" for five or ten minutes straight when getting knotted, and the idea of that rather irritated me.

Gods, they were all so boring. Pretty, yes, as all Zilly Omegas were, but damn those vapid, long-lashed looks they gave me. I'd rather just fuck them hard, in and out, and avoid locking us up anyway.

I wore the thick silver around the base of my cock during all my Burns, and that made my cock look fuller, harder. The metal gleamed against my brown skin.

Chichi craned his head around his shoulder, watching me finish taking off my clothes. He wiggled his ass, then reached back to rub himself lightly, his fingers coming away with his own clear slick. An Omega's slick wasn't in endless supply, so later we'd need the lube, but not now. Not for this first fuck.

His eyes widened as I kicked my pants aside and cocked my hip, my erection bobbing straight out from my body.

"You're so big. And so handsome. Please. Put it in me now. I can't wait."

He sounded sincere enough. An Omega who was experienced, and who loved sex. That's how they were trained at all the chattel farms. To love sex. To revere it.

Father taught me they were perfect holes for us Alphas, made for us to service our Burns and bear our young. That was their purpose in life. And he wasn't wrong.

Zilly's was a high-end farm. Expensive. Catered to the wealthy like me. Like my father, Varian Vandergale, and my litter-mate, Trigg. All Zilly's Omegas were impeccable. Lovely.

The Omega who bore me had come from this farm. I never knew him. Father had signed a contract for the birth to be a closed deal, the records sealed. The Omega had no right to his litter after we were born. My brothers, Trigg, Kris, and I were raised as Alphas by our Alpha parent. And our Omega father, after giving birth, was sent far away to another farm so that Father might never again accidentally run into him.

Father had other litters, too, all planned, all from different Omegas. My litter was in the middle. I was one of triplets. My younger brothers, thirteen years younger, were twins, Bren and Mica. My older brothers, whom I'd never met, were another set of triplets, and were thirty years my senior.

I was raised to believe Omegas were purposed only to bear our families and discarded afterward. Sure, I'd heard about bondmates, but they seemed rare.

Honestly, I didn't like kids and never wanted them, not by marriage, and not Father's way, either. And an Omega bondmate seemed like more trouble than it was worth. I liked my independence.

The Omega who posed naked in front of me right now was good for one thing and one thing only. Good sex and cooling down my Burn.

I walked toward him, reaching out to touch the side of his hip. His skin was smooth. Soft. My cock twitched as I looked down at the shine of his slick on his crack. His thighs trembled a little.

"Kneel on the bed," I said.

8

"Of course." He immediately climbed up, pressing his ass higher in the air and his head down until his chin touched the mattress.

That was better. I was taller than my brothers and Father. Broader, too. The Omega kneeling on the bed was the perfect height for me to fuck standing up. I preferred it. Less body contact.

I wasn't out of my mind with the Burn yet. So I wanted to start out with the least of bodily entanglements.

I ran my forefinger down Chichi's crack.

He sighed in pleasure, then said, "You don't have to wait. My body is ready."

I palmed his cheeks apart. His hole was small, not stretched. I rolled my eyes at his impatience. He was horny. He wanted it. But I hated when there was blood. It was so inconvenient.

I said, "Hold on."

I speared him with a finger. He easily accepted it so I added another. Then a third.

When I took them away, his hole gaped.

I pressed at the dark emptiness with the head of my steel hard cock.

"Yes!" Chichi hissed.

I pushed in slowly, wanting to feel every inch of myself go into him. I didn't think much about his pleasure, but he cried out, "More, more!"

My cock was like a dark pole going into him. Poking inside him, getting used to his tightness and heat and slick. It felt so good.

Soon I was ramming into him and his cries filled the room. I made no sounds. I didn't yell or squeal or scream. I was an Alpha. I'd been raised by a respectable family.

I plunged into him all the way to my silver cock ring, over and over. I touched his hips only to pull him tighter to me. Faster and faster I fucked.

I came hard and fast, the Burn washing pleasure through me. Instead of subsiding, the pleasure took hold and gripped me and did not let up for quite some time. I came three more times before pulling out.

Chichi sounded like he came several times, too, but I didn't ask.

I pulled out and wiped myself on a towel. I grabbed some water from a small fridge by the bed and drank the whole thing.

Chichi grabbed some water as well, before presenting his cool mouth to my erection as I continued to stand by the side of the bed.

My cock throbbed and I came in his very experienced mouth. He sucked me hard and there was so much fluid it dribbled from his lips before he could swallow it all.

Finally, I needed to lie down. I crawled onto the bed where Chichi seated himself on me and did most of the work while I mostly dozed, then came again.

Later, we ate cold sandwiches from the fridge and napped. I'd come five times.

When night fell, we did it all again.

Sometimes Chichi tried to get me to talk, or to hold him. But I had no interest in that. He was nothing to me. Just a body. A hole.

I spent two days at Zilly's before I was ready to leave. An exhausted Chichi thanked me for a good time.

I said, "Yes, yes," perhaps a little too impatiently and his sweet mouth turned down as he left out a side door to the interior of the farm.

I exited the mating room into a hall where, on a weird impulse, so unlike me, I passed by the paybox and left a generous tip. Chichi wouldn't get the money, but he'd be allowed to pick a present for himself from any online source: makeup, jewelry, whatever he wanted.

I don't know why I left the gift. It was such a gods damned ordinary Burn.

10

When I walked outside, the light was blinding. A stabbing pain hit my eyes. I slid my sunglasses from their satin case and put them on. I pushed back tiny wisps of my black hair that had come loose from my thick braid. Combing them behind my ears, I made sure my braid was tight, my hair slick as a cap against my scalp.

When I could see, I noticed Trigg's red Porsche to my left. It was law that after a Burn all Alphas had to wait twenty-four hours before they could drive. I usually got a cab home. But sometimes Trigg would have Zilly's notify him when I was ready to leave, and meet me. Obviously, this time he'd been keeping tabs on me. That was how litter-mates were. Well, sometimes.

The muscles around my eyes and jaw tightened at the thought. That was how *some* litter-mates were. Kris and I never spoke, hadn't since we'd been eighteen. Twelve years of silence. A long, long time. Trigg visited Kris often and kept me up to date. I still pretended not to care.

I walked around the car and lowered myself into the passenger seat.

Trigg barely looked at me, but when he spoke, his words were soft. "Hey, Math. How was it this time?"

"Fine."

"Just fine?"

"Yep."

"Did you ever knot this time?"

"None of your business."

Trigg was the only one who knew I didn't knot. I led him to believe it was on purpose, that I chose not to.

When I had told him about it a couple years ago, he'd been shocked.

"But it's the best part. All Alphas love it."

"Sure," I'd said. "But who wants to be stuck inside a boring Omega for that long? I can just keep fucking him and come again and again. It's the same thing."

"It's not the same thing," Trigg had said.

11

"Shut the fuck up. You don't know everything." But his words exemplified my difference. That I wasn't normal. I kept telling myself it wasn't that big a deal. It wasn't everything. Who cared? Not me.

Sure, my friends talked about it, but my friends also tended to be blowhards and they exaggerated an awful lot. I had many young Alpha friends who talked big and loud. They were funny and fun, but I barely believed fifty percent of what they said.

Surely there were a lot of Alphas like me who would agree they despised the closeness of knotting. Who wanted to be touched all the time? Who wanted to be so close like that that you breathed each other's air?

"So," Trigg said, pulling onto the highway where the fields of the farm passed by, green and fresh, smelling of alfalfa. "Are you hungry or am I taking you directly home?"

"You can drop me at work."

"Work? No way, Math. You should relax for the rest of today."

"I slept in the mating room this morning."

"How many hours?"

"Two."

Trigg snorted. "Let's go for a steak lunch. Then I'm taking you home."

He always knew what I was feeling, even when I was being a dick. My litter-mate Trigg knew my every mood: hungry, angry, jealous, tired, and even my most secret resentments. Things I never spoke of. Thoughts I denied. About Kris. About our upbringing. About bondmates and family.

All that thinking. It was a waste of energy. But Trigg didn't need me to speak to know me. We'd shared an Omega womb together. We'd come from the same seed and the same environment. He knew me all too well. And so did Kris, who I didn't want to think about. Who I didn't want to see ever again.

"No argument," Trigg pushed gently. "Food, then home, ok?" He was a good brother to me. Better than I deserved. And I *was* extremely hungry. Yeah, I could eat. And sleep.

"Fine," I said, and glowered out the side window at the forest that started to appear as the car smoothly climbed up the mountain and out of the valley.

Chapter Two

Saber

"Daddy, daddy!" Tybor came running into the office.

I'd left my five-year-old twins watching TV while I decided today was the day I was going to try to sort all the bills my bondmate had left me with after his death.

Tybor rammed into my knees as I swiveled the desk chair toward him to see what had him so bothered. With an awkward scramble, he climbed heavily into my lap, the palm of his hand pressing hard on my slightly convex stomach, making me grunt.

I grabbed him around the waist and hefted him into a more comfortable position. He peered up at me with big, ocean-blue eyes, his blond curls catching the light and turning slightly pink against his forehead.

"Luke called me a meega again. You said you didn't like it. So he shouldn't say it."

Out the corner of my eye, I saw Luke, the Alpha twin, peer around the threshold of the door, but I pretended he wasn't there. Little Tybor was the Omega twin, and he was only just learning what that label meant to him and to the outside world. I didn't like to think that life would be harder for him, and I was trying to teach both my boys that labels didn't make us who we were inside, that we were all of value and our little family needed to be loyal always and support one another. But the real world did not usually reflect my idealistic notions.

"The word is Omega, honey," I said softly to him. "And you're right, he shouldn't call you that. He should use your name. Tybor."

"But we're the same," Tybor said. "We look exactly alike. Why isn't he om meega, too?"

I put my chin down so it touched his head and drew in his scent. Chocolate and oranges. My beautiful

14

baby Omega was so sweet. "Because that's just the way you were made. Some of us are made Omega and some Alpha."

"I choose Alpha," said Tybor.

"Sometimes we don't get a choice in some things."

He thumped his little fist against my thigh and pouted. "I could pretend."

"Why, sweetheart?"

"I want to be like Luke in *every* way."

"You're beautiful just the way you are."

One side of Tybor's mouth curved up, suppressing a grin.

Just then Luke stepped into the room. His lips pressed tight with worry. His cheeks were puffed a little as if he wanted to speak but didn't know what to say.

I held out my arm to him. He came forward and let me embrace him around the shoulders. His head was down. He smelled of fire and the sea.

"And Luke, too, is beautiful just the way he is."

Tybor pressed his cheek against my chest. I felt him nod.

Luke twisted in my hold and bent his head back, catching my gaze. "Daddy, why can't I say Omega if it's not telling a lie?"

"Because you both have perfectly good names. And it is respectful to another to use his name."

"What do spectful mean?" asked Tybor.

"Respectful means you treat another person the way you wish to be treated. It means you think about your words hard before you speak them. It means if you don't have anything nice to say, it might be better not to speak at all."

My little speech was probably going to be forgotten in ten minutes. My sons would continue to play and fight, laugh and yell and tease each other. Of course that was healthy, but I was determined to raise them as good men, as equals regardless of what the world thought about gender differences.

"But is Omega a bad word?" asked Luke.

"No. But if you use the word to point out your differences like you're trying to put him down or make fun of him, then it can be."

"I wasn't, Daddy," Luke tried to argue.

"But Tybor got upset, right?" I hugged Luke tighter.

"I don't know."

"I think he did."

Tybor pushed away from my chest so he could look at Luke. "I broke his fire truck."

"You did?" I asked.

Both boys nodded solemnly.

"I'm sorry, Daddy," said Tybor.

"I'm sorry, too," said Luke.

I got up, swinging them both in my arms before setting them to the floor.

"Okay, kiddos, let's go see if we can fix it."

Their faces instantly lit up and from one minute to the next it was as if nothing bad had ever happened.

*

Drayden, my Alpha, died on the same day I found out I was almost three months pregnant.

He was hardly ever home except for his Burns, an airline pilot always on the go. When he was home, he stayed to himself and barely tolerated our twin sons. Over the past two years, except for his Burns, we had taken to sleeping in separate rooms.

Our bond had been quick and formal, but I was smitten at first. I thought Drayden loved me when what he had really needed was a child-bearer and a maid and a convenient hole for his Burns.

Our mate-bond, what I felt of it, was weak when I compared it to what I had learned about bondmates. Raised on a chattel farm, I'd met Drayden when he'd rented me for one of his Burns. He'd knotted me into total ecstasy and he decided right after that I would be a good partner and give him healthy children.

He dated me for about two weeks before I said yes to his offer of marriage.

I was naïve. I thought the bond, when we formed it, would make me fall in love with him. It didn't. I cared about him, but I didn't ever feel that surge some people talked about when they could actually feel their mate inside their mind and know if they were happy, sad, hurt or… dead.

When Drayden died I never felt a twinge of it through our weak bond. No pain. No fear. No shock or dread. Just over three months ago, his plane went down in the ocean with fifty-seven passengers, all lost, and the investigation into why the accident happened with all the safety regs in place was still ongoing.

Drayden was an experienced pilot with awards and over eleven thousand hours in the cockpit of many different kinds of planes.

I remember thinking at the time that it was impossible that Drayden was dead. There must have been some mistake. He was expert at what he did. He'd never lost a passenger even in the worst weather conditions. He never lost his cool. He was a rational, meticulous thinker. If the plane went down with Drayden at the controls, then it had to be for a reason he couldn't control, like a bomb or a flock of birds, or human error on the maintenance level.

I remembered that day very clearly, the phone call to notify me, the chill I'd felt all over my skin at the news, a chill that took over all except for a tiny flame in my belly where twin fetuses were starting to grow. I didn't know they were twins yet—a second set to match my beautiful Luke and Tybor—it had been too early, and of course I couldn't really feel them. But the heat there, and knowing I carried new life conceived of Drayden's blood, his DNA, made me begin to tremble so hard I had to sit down.

I never shed a tear for Drayden, but that didn't mean I didn't grieve him in my own way. I lost sleep over my inability to have felt his death. I worried about being an Omega left alone to care for our growing family. I dreamed every night for a month that it had all been a clerical error, and it wasn't really Drayden on that flight. In my dreams, he walked through the front door in his usual manner, quiet and reserved, hanging his pilot coat in the closet, removing his shoes, and going straight to his office with barely a hello in greeting.

Our sons cried at the news, confused and upset. But young as they were, they adapted quickly to Drayden's absence, since they barely knew their Alpha father and had bonded mainly to me. For the first few weeks, they'd ask me questions like if I was sure their Alpha daddy was never coming home, and where did I think people went after they died.

But after a while, their behavior normalized.

For me, my grief might have been minimal but my worry wasn't.

Drayden had left behind a large life insurance policy and some decent bank accounts. They were in my name as well, but as a newly single Omega, I wasn't allowed to have financial accounts without an Alpha signatory. I was allowed access for the first few weeks, the same as it had been when Drayden was alive, but now the bank was sending me notices. My withdrawals would be suspended and my funds put on hold if I didn't hire an Alpha financial guardian to help me with my affairs.

The bank's letters were oh so polite, telling me their policies were for my own protection, my own good, and to make sure my money was safe. There was wording like: *You need not worry about things you are unequipped to handle, and if you cannot find a financial guardian on your own, we can provide this service for a monthly fee that is commensurate with your spending.*

Every letter I got like that, I ripped to shreds. They were there to protect my money, they said. Except from themselves, since they were quite willing to take it in order to provide me with their guardian service.

Drayden had kept me away from all his Alpha friends. We rarely socialized. I never knew my parents or any siblings I might have had. And I didn't want my in-laws bothered with any of it. They saw their grandkids once in a while, but that was the extent of our relationship. I had no one who could help me outside of the bank itself. They had me between a rock and a hard place.

So when the bank called me to set up a meeting, I was a bit curt. Maybe even rude. A financial guardianship from them meant every monetary expenditure I had from now on would be monitored and scrutinized and could actually be denied if found to be frivolous or excessive.

"I'll have you know, my Alpha was barely ever home," I said. "I handled all the household duties, including finances and all the bills myself. I don't need the help."

"Yes, very well, I'm sure you're right," said the Alpha on the other end of the line. "But our bank policy is there to insure the safety of all our customers. We want you to have the best experience, and not have to worry your pretty little head about--"

"Excuse me?" I interrupted. "Maybe your *pretty little head* needs to stop worrying about whether or not I am pretty and listen. I've been doing this for years. My bondmate traveled for his job."

I heard the Alpha clear his throat. "Still, your husband was the main signatory, as deemed by law. All these facts can be discussed at the meeting. And now," he continued without taking a breath. "Would morning or afternoon be better for you?"

I could fume about it until I burst into flames and it wouldn't help. This was the world, fair or not. It infuriated me mainly for my sons. Little Tybor was never going to get all the freedoms his brother Luke could take for granted.

I took a deep breath and let it out in a hiss, making sure the Alpha heard me. The boys were up by 6:30 am every day. They hadn't started kindergarten yet.

"Mornings," I replied through gritted teeth.

"Very well. Is tomorrow, nine-thirty a.m. Wednesday the twelfth all right?"

"That will be fine!"

"I thank you for doing business with Journey Bank, and have a nice--"

I hung up before he could finish.

The next morning I had the boys freshly bathed and dressed in time for our outing. I styled my straight, blond hair away from my face and behind my ears, and wore my best suit, though I wasn't sure why I bothered. We were going to be discussing *my* money. I should have been able to show up in a ripped t-shirt and jeans if I wanted.

I strapped the boys into the backseat of the minivan and off we went.

Ten minutes later we pulled into the parking garage of the bank, which was located in a two-story building in the middle of the city.

For a long moment, after turning off the engine, I sat and did nothing.

Finally, Luke said, "Daddy, are we getting out here?"

"Yes, baby. I just needed to take a minute to be quiet and think."

"Okay, Daddy," he said softly.

It infuriated me that I had to do this meeting, but I knew if I went inside in my current mood it would just make matters worse. I took deep breaths. I forced my fists to unclench.

When I felt ready, my muscles relaxed and my breathing calmed, I undid my seatbelt and opened the driver's side door.

I got out and slid the passenger door back, reaching in, undoing the twins' seatbelts on their car seats, and helping them out.

They looked so cute standing side by side, mirror images of each other, Alpha to Omega, wearing their little suits with cut-off pants and knee high socks with their best black shoes.

"Now," I said, waggling my finger at them. "You two stay close to my side at all times. Hold hands. And no running around. Use your inside voice, okay?"

"Okay, Daddy," they replied in unison.

Together, walking through the gray and rust shadows of the parking structure, we strolled through the entrance of Journey Bank.

Chapter Three

Mathias

"I totally need this favor, Mathias," said the voice on the phone. "The meeting's at 9:30 and I can't make it."

Cord was not really my friend, but we'd shared some meals and gone to some parties together, and I guess maybe all that meant more to him. He worked downstairs. I was upper management. Upper *upper* management.

"Guardianships aren't my area," I said. "I'm on the Board for fuck's sake. Get your ass in here and do your job!"

"I've got too much on my plate."

"I know. Your new Omega lover." I rolled my eyes.

Cord had been coming to me more and more lately, asking if he could go home early, or come in to work later than his schedule demanded.

"We're bonding and it's affecting my Burn schedule."

"So why talk to me? Go to HR and fill out the required forms for time off."

"I will, but right now, I have this meeting."

"Cancel it."

"I can't. The Omega who needs a signatory has let this slide until his deadline is up. He could lose access to all his accounts and he's got little ones."

I sighed. "It means a lot of follow up because if I sign on this account it's my name on the line. I can't just change it on a whim to your signature. It'll take tons of legal forms."

"It's an easy case. I swear. And you're good at all that. It's a no-brainer for you. The Omega says he's been handling the household bills already for years. You won't need to do much. He just needs an Alpha to sign off. It'll be paperwork that's maybe twice a month. That's it."

"That's it, you say? Huh. You behave as if you think I have no life."

"I swear if you cover for me I'll do anything you want. Anything."

"Anything?" I raised my left eyebrow and leaned back in my desk chair. Certainly I had the time. My job was mostly a show of power. My father owned the bank. He liked to keep a family presence there. I was his flashy mouthpiece, the guy who stood around looking important and making employees nervous.

"Anything," he said a little breathlessly.

But mostly I took long lunches and played video games on my office computer because my workload was definitely not full-time. If I did a guy a favor, it was for a price. Father taught me to be ruthless that way. I saw nothing wrong with that.

"I'll hold you to that *anything*," I said.

"Thank you, Mathias. Thank you so much! I'm emailing you all the docs right now."

I hung up before he could embarrass himself even more. The dude was so in love it was irritating.

I glanced at the clock. It was nine-twenty. Great. Nothing like waiting until the last minute. Cord had no sense.

I had ten minutes to prepare. As his email came in, I saw the file size was pretty big. Damn him.

I had to get some paperwork together as well as printouts of this Omega's accounts. Seriously, Cord was going to pay for this.

By the time I headed downstairs, I was already five minutes late and my phone beeper was going off.

I ignored it as the elevator doors opened, depositing me in the bank's shiny, marble-floored foyer.

I saw him right away. The Omega who needed a guardian because of the untimely death of his Alpha. He was the only Omega in the vast space of the bank's first floor, looking small and out of place with two identical children, one on either side of him holding his hands.

Great. Cord was really going to owe me now. He didn't tell me the guy was bringing his litter. With the exception of my little brothers, who were both just about to turn eighteen, I had no patience for kids.

I let out an annoyed breath and quickly approached the little family.

"Saber Volmar?"

The Omega looked up quickly, eyes hard, wary. His sons gazed at me with big eyes and tilted heads. They both looked like him, but from their scents, I could immediately tell they were mirror twins. One was an Alpha and one an Omega, unlike my little brothers who were both Alphas. In mirror twins, the Omega was usually a leftie, and in many even their organs were reversed inside their bodies.

I knew this because of Bren and Mica and their weird identical twin thing. Though I was a triplet, my litter mates and I were not identical in any way.

The Omega dad did not answer my question outright. He said, "You're not the guy I talked to on the phone."

"No. He had an emergency. So you're dealing with me." With an Alpha, I would hold out my hand and introduce myself. But I didn't deal with Omegas much except during my Burn.

Saber Volmar was a dark blond with severe hazel eyes that seared right through me.

"I can come back," he said.

A sweet lilac scent floated about me and as I inhaled, my pulse quickened. I'd just come out of my Burn so I shouldn't have responded that way. It wasn't that I didn't have sexual encounters outside the Burn, simply it was a fact that my sex drive diminished for several days afterward. The oddness of the sensation took me back for a second. I swallowed hard, focusing on the task at hand.

"Ah, but you see, you can't reschedule. You were sent several notices by this bank which you ignored. You're running out of time before your accounts are frozen. It takes time to undo that sort of thing, so it seems you're in desperate need of financial guardianship."

"And that would be you?" The question was asked with a tone of accusation.

Suddenly, the tiny Omega at his side stepped forward gazing up at me and asked, "Is all of this yours?"

I frowned down at him. "I don't live here, if that's what you mean."

Saber tugged on his son's hand, pulling him back. "Shh, Tybor," he said.

It felt utterly wrong to be talking to two Omegas in the front lobby of the bank. Or anywhere for that matter.

I looked up at Saber's hard gaze. "If you'd like to follow me to my office where we can conduct our business in privacy."

Saber's nostrils flared slightly, letting me know he was not happy.

Who cared? It'd all be done in a half hour or less and I'd be rid of them, with only a bit of paperwork to review a couple times a month.

Again, the lilac fragrance drifted over me. Nothing too weird, or that I hated, but the responses from my body included a prickling of my skin and a strange hardening inside that felt like it was forming in the center of my ribcage.

It unnerved me because the only time I'd ever felt a response like that was when my brother Kris's scent had changed when he and I and Trigg turned eighteen. It had made me feel crazy and out of control, violent, in fact, and all the resentments I'd had toward him of Father favoring him, calling him his perfect, golden Alpha child multiplied. I hated what he'd become. I hated even more that I was attracted in all the wrong ways toward him.

Never had I told a soul about the evil things I'd said to my own litter-mate, or about my threats toward Kris, and my disowning of him as my brother. No one knew the real reasons why. Trigg suspected, though, without me having to say a word.

But now wasn't the time to be thinking about that bullshit.

For several seconds, we didn't move.

"Well?" asked Saber.

I blinked the world back into focus. "This way."

I turned and led the little group to the elevators. As we all clambered in, Tybor pulled back. "I don't wanna."

"It's okay, baby," Saber said to him. "It's just a little car that takes us to the upper level."

"Kid's never been on an elevator before?" I asked.

Saber ignored me. "Hold my hand tight, okay?"

Tybor nodded, stepping up to his father's side.

When the doors closed, Tybor buried his face in his father's hip. Saber let go of his hand and put his arm around the kid's shoulders, then stared straight ahead.

The other kid, the little Alpha who had remained silent the whole time, stared up at me now. He had his father's eyes, but darker blue, almost cobalt. He smelled of salt and wind. The Alpha was strong in that one. I glanced away, thinking to myself that I hoped they stayed quiet so this meeting would go by smoothly.

When we exited the elevator onto the second floor, our footfalls were cushioned by thick, high end purple carpet. The walls gleamed white with purple trim. My door was ajar, purple with a gold plaque embossed with my name.

As we walked up to it, Saber said, without inflection, "Mathias Vandergale."

Since I hadn't really introduced myself, I figured now was as good a time as any. "The one and only."

"Your father owns this bank."

Well, well, the Omega had done his homework.

"One of two owners, but my father has the greater share," I replied.

"And you're going to be financial guardian to my deceased Alpha's estate?"

"So it seems."

His mouth opened and his face paled a bit making his lips look pinker and his eyes brighter. As we entered my office, I heard him gasp out softly, "Why?"

"It's one of our services," I replied. I motioned to a couch on one wall. "Your sons can sit there while we conduct business. They're not going to be a problem, are they?"

At once, Tybor let go of his father's hand and ran to the couch, but his eyes were on a table beside the couch where I kept a bowl of colorfully wrapped, hard candy.

I waved at the bowl. "They can have some if it will help keep them quiet."

Saber turned to look at what I was pointing at. He frowned. "One piece each, you hear?"

The Alpha boy let go of Saber's other hand and joined his brother. They both looked up at their father, respectfully nodding.

When Saber nodded back, they turned to the bowl and took their time choosing the color they each wanted.

When they were seated and unwrapping their goodies, I motioned Saber to a chair in front of my desk where I'd had my secretary bring in the forms and new pens for signing. Then I went behind my desk and sat, opening my laptop and bringing up all the accounts in question.

"I see here your Alpha, Drayden Volmar, has left you some reasonable sums which, when combined with what the life insurance pays, will help take you a long way in raising your children."

"He was a very organized and efficient Alpha who earned a good salary," said Saber coolly. "My children and I were well provided for."

"If you invest properly, and it is my duty to see that you do, you will be fine for many years, decades even, or until you are bonded to another Alpha."

I heard a sound like a snort and looked up.

Saber's mouth was twisted. His hazel eyes were dark gray-green now, and he was clearly angry. His emotion brought a delightful flush to his cheeks. The set of his body and the tightness in his jaw line drew my attention into an almost hyper-focus. Saber was like a piece of lightning momentarily caught in a dark room, startling everything with its brilliance.

I opened my mouth to question his response but before I could say anything, Saber said, "I can take care of myself! I don't need *you* to see to my proper investments. If I want to take all my money out at once and spend it at a casino, I should be able to!"

Clearly, his irrationality was the result of something else. I told myself he was probably still in grief, even as I marveled at his forward manner. All the Omegas I'd ever known had been taught to be sweet, polite, demure. And sexual.

"That would be unwise," I said. "And that's why I'm here assigned to your case."

Saber sat up straighter and crossed his arms in front of his chest.

"Are you going to tell me where, when and what I can spend *my* money on, then? What color underwear I should own? How much I should spend on my kids at Christmas? The brand of diapers for my future babies?"

"Well, we're getting a little ahead of ourselves here, aren't we?" I asked.

He glowered through half-closed eyelids. "I have two more on the way."

"You're pregnant?"

He nodded tightly.

I glanced again at his accounts, pretending not to sniff the air to see if I could smell it on him, along with those wonderful lilacs. There was nothing, but then he was hiding it well with his shirt a bit loose and maybe that lilac aroma was a cologne.

"Do you currently have medical insurance?"

28

He said, thin-lipped, "Through Drayden's company."

"You should be fine, then. Although if that insurance isn't for life--"

"The insurance lasts until the last of Drayden's children are eighteen. Then I have the option to buy into the group policy."

I leaned back, again surprised. This Omega was not what I expected. Most Omegas I knew needed Alphas to help and guide them. "I see you've done your homework."

Saber rolled his eyes at me, which caused me to puff my chest out a little.

I decided to get straight to business. "Your expenditures are mainly your house and utilities, a few credit cards and food. Do you have a car?"

"Owned and paid for."

"Owned by your Alpha, no doubt. We'll have to see about getting it put into a trust, along with the house, so all of it is under your name but with the bank as signatory."

Saber opened his mouth as if to make another smart remark.

I cut him off. "It's for your own protection. So no one can take it from you like your deceased Alpha's relatives, or someone unscrupulous enough to scam it out from under you. Omegas on their own can never be too safe."

My explanation shut him up. For the moment.

I scrolled his files for more details.

"Your house payment is pretty high. I see its worth is a bit more than your standard of living should be now that you're an Omega on your own. Have you thought about moving?"

Saber blinked. "What?"

"To somewhere more affordable?"

A pained look crossed his face. Something inside me I rarely felt gave a twinge in response.

Fuck, I didn't give one shit about this guy. To prove to myself I didn't care, I added, "And you are raising an Omega child, which is not required. Wouldn't it be better if he was brought up with his kind? You know, like a farm where they know how to train them, how to make them be the best Omegas they can be. It would save you money in the long run, too."

As I saw his face pale in a combination of fear and revulsion, my brother Kris flashed in my mind. A memory of how he'd given me the same look so many years ago.

I was not one to mince words. I stated the obvious. So what if people got offended? That was their problem. But now I remembered Kris's look of horror when I'd spoken cruel words in anger, in jealousy, and an uncomfortable burning started in my chest.

"Excuse me, but you are probably the rudest Alpha I have ever met!" Saber's hands gripped the arms of his chair hard, and he started to stand.

I was really going to fuck with Cord when all this was said and done. I didn't need this bullshit.

"Can I request a different guardian, please? All I need is an Alpha to sign on the account, then give me access, not someone who will question everything I do!"

Had Saber met many Alphas?

"Please sit back down, Mister Volmar. It's not my intent to question everything you do. But it is my job to make smart financial suggestions. That's all I was saying."

"Well, your suggestions are highly offensive!" But Saber sat. Formal. Stiff. And the lilac scent grew stronger. I couldn't help but breathe deeply of it.

The two identical boys on the couch sat very still and solemn, watching us, eyes wide. I wondered how much they even understood what was going on.

Well, at least they weren't running around screaming and out of control. The imps clearly loved their father and obeyed him. I conceded that maybe it had been none of my business at the very least to suggest Saber get rid of one of them. If his Alpha, when he'd been alive, had wanted to raise an Omega child, who was I to argue with that decision?

"All right, all right. We can clearly cross that suggestion off the list then. It's my job to give you the options, that's all," I said. "No offense intended."

"I still want to request another guardian."

"There are none to be had right now. The bank has assigned you to me. But you can certainly put it in writing to change guardians. The bank takes six weeks to review the claim."

My voice didn't sound right to me. It was rough-edged, wavering. The air around us felt suddenly electric and dangerous.

"You can be sure I will do that," Saber said. "Now, what do I have to do today to keep my access? And how much will you restrict it? Are there guidelines, or is it at your discretion?"

I decided I was done playing roles. Done arguing with sweet-scented Omegas who thought they knew all. It wasn't my job. I lifted my hands and shrugged.

"I'm not going to interfere with you. Is that what you wanted to hear? It's not worth the drama. This job is below my pay grade anyway. So, I'll sign off on your expenditures, whatever you want without question. You seem like you're fully capable of figuring out your own finances."

Saber took a deep breath. His head lowered and his eyes glared as though he was waiting for the catch.

I quickly tried to find some middle ground. Obviously, neither of us wanted to be at this meeting. "Look, this is wasting your time and mine. Do we at least agree on that one thing?"

"Agreed." Saber's voice was curt. Harsh.

I glanced again at my screen. He really was in decent financial shape.

"There's a home inspection required, but I'll waive that, too. Even though it's for your own protection, to make sure you are allotted sufficient funds, if you have them, to maintain your assets, but no problem." I flicked a button on my keyboard. "It's waived."

"You make it sound like I'm trying to hide something," Saber said.

"What? No. I'm merely trying to meet you on middle ground here."

"Well, I don't have anything to hide. I just want to raise my children in peace and in the lifestyle Drayden set up for us."

"I understand that." I spoke slowly, wondering why he was arguing. I had just given in to him on, well, everything. It wasn't like me, but I wanted this done and out of my hair.

"But you said my house was too expensive."

Yeah, and I had suggested he let go of one of his sons, too. Backtracking, I said, "For now, you are solid. Is that what you wanted to hear?"

"It's not about what I *want* to hear. If you're the financial guardian, then it's your job to tell me if I can't afford something. Do I or do I not have enough?"

"You have enough."

"For now, you said."

This Omega was tough. "Yes, I said that. That's because I don't know what your expenditures will be down the line. And do you want your Alpha children to go to college? Do you enjoy wearing designer suits? It's simply what we put into the equation, nothing personal."

"But everything about this is personal."

I shook my head. I wanted this done and him gone.

Saber sat forward now, his elbows on his knees. "Tell me," he said, "that you wouldn't feel it was personal if someone came along and froze your access to your accounts and decided to count out every penny to you for every expenditure. Tell me the truth." Then he added, with a little hiss. "Alpha."

The boys on the couch both opened their mouths in shock, as if they'd been taught the word was a curse or something. I heard one whisper to the other, "Daddy called him that word."

I kept my eyes steady on Saber.

"You have no idea, do you?" Saber continued. "What it's like to be a non-Alpha in an Alpha run world. Nor do you probably care, but if you have an ounce of heart, you would see that if your bank really wants to help, if they want to help me, a lowly Omega--"

The boys gasped again.

"You might do it with at least a tiny bit of compassion for how that might feel to me."

Lilacs and fresh summer rivers. My brothers and I used to go to camp every summer, our only time away from Father's authority and piercing gazes and his strict teachings of how to be a proper Alpha. Trigg, Kris and I looked forward to it every year. Freedom from a kind of tyranny my mind still wrapped me up with. Father's voice always in my ear. Never good enough. Never as golden and strong as Kris. Never book-smart and artistic like Trigg.

I did know what it was like not to be free. Even as an adult Alpha, Father's strong ties still bound me.

Compassion? Where did that get me?

Saber was watching me as if trying to read me. I'd lost my train of thought. I couldn't even remember what we'd just been talking about. Something about this being personal?

My skin was hot all of a sudden. And Saber, a mere Omega, looked more put-together than I felt—than I had felt in a long time. He looked trim and fit and contained, his pale, slicked-back hair flashing in the light, his chin up, his posture ramrod straight, and his kids sucking on their candies and as still and quiet as timid little birds.

He was nothing like my own father. He probably hugged his kids for fun. He probably laughed at their stupid jokes and didn't correct them with a hand or a switch.

My breath caught as resentment snarled through me.

"Well," I said, trying to distract myself from uncomfortable thoughts. "Where were we? Oh yes, the house inspection. Did I not say it's fine? It's waived."

Letting out a breath of frustration, Saber said, "I said I don't have anything to hide. You make it sound like I do, that I'm stupid or something. Go ahead. If it's policy, send someone out. I'm fine with it."

I blinked. "That person would not be someone. It would be me." It was the last thing I wanted, but rules were rules.

"Fine," he said. "Just don't insult me, okay?"

I opened my mouth to argue, but what was the point? This beautiful, perfect-father Omega was infuriating.

"I'll print everything out now, and we'll get to the signatures. It will only be a few more minutes."

"Good." Saber crossed his arms again and leaned back, turning his head away as if he wanted no more of this conversation.

I couldn't decide if he looked more beautiful head on, or in profile. His blond hair seemed to reflect all the softer colors in the room. Though most of the room was black, white and chrome, his locks absorbed the pinks and golds of the early daylight coming through the window, and the soft bluish purple of the carpet at our feet.

The printer beeped in the corner of the room and I got up to gather the paperwork.

I handed Saber one of my best pens and he scooted closer to the desk as I showed him where to initial and sign as I explained everything he was seeing.

When we both focused on the task, our tempers evened out and the energy in the room changed. We were in sync. He had few questions and he agreed to everything when I assured him he wasn't being ripped off and I myself would see to it he had the best accounts with the highest interest rates.

It was very strange that I suddenly felt the intense urge to reassure him at every step. It was just a job and I didn't care much for it except the perks were good and Father paid me an embarrassing salary. But for this Omega who should have meant nothing to me, I experienced a kind of reality change. I felt bigger, as if the room were too small to contain me. And when I leaned forward to show him certain items within the documents, my hearing became more sensitive. His breaths sounded as if they were in my ears. When his hand moved the pen to sign at the dotted lines, the soft, rolling sound it made was almost erotic.

The suit he wore was black, fairly plain with a white shirt underneath. But the tie kept catching my eye. Lavender. Silk. I decided lavender was my favorite color. I'd never had a favorite color before.

The two boys on the couch whispered together and giggled. Normally I saw children as a distraction, nothing more. But they didn't bother me at all, in that moment.

Everything felt as if it was in the right place, normal, steady, even serene.

As Saber bent to sign the last document, the pen shining in his hand, I was so intent on him that I forgot myself for a few seconds. I didn't breathe. I didn't move. My body trembled from a place deep inside that suddenly made itself known, as if gasping, shuddering, coming to life.

It was as if I had never truly breathed, but always held myself back, always tense, resentful that others seemed to feel and respond to things I couldn't. As a kid I'd been the jealous joker. The loudmouth. The one who made light of everyone and everything.

It was funny, actually. I had nothing to be bitter about as an adult. Except maybe I had wished that Father loved me best.

"Anything else?" Saber's voice startled me out of my weird daydream.

"What?"

"Is there anything else?" he asked again, eyebrows coming together in confusion.

"No." I gathered the papers and straightened them.

"So this is it. Things will resume as they have been. I have access, though limited."

I glanced up and my face heated just to meet his eyes which made me feel foolish and young.

"I won't limit you myself unless I see something that is extreme. You seem to have a handle on your life, as you said. But if you still want to petition for another guardian, you have that right."

He sat back, contemplating me. "You still need to do a home visit, right?"

"I don't see that there's a need." But now I really wanted to see where he lived. I was curious, and damned if I knew why.

"But if you think it's too extravagant for our needs." He hesitated. "I want my kids to go to college. Both of them."

I raised an eyebrow at that. The Omega twin would have few choices on that pathway to higher education.

"And the ones on the way," he added.

How had I forgotten? He had said he was pregnant with twins. Could that be the reason my body responded to strangely? Was he giving off bizarre pheromones into the air?

"When would be convenient for you?" I asked.

"Tomorrow. Any time, really. Honestly, I don't want to have to move, but maybe I can re-finance, or you might have some other ideas. This is your job, after all, right?"

It wasn't, really. But I had training and I was rather a genius with finances. With numbers and money.

I nodded.

"Morning or afternoon?" I asked.

He shrugged and the gesture made me almost smile. "I'm not going anywhere."

"Around eleven, then?"

"That will be fine." Saber rose. He did not hold his hand out for me to shake it, and I didn't expect him to.

The kids slid off the couch and ran to his side. I got up and walked them all to the door.

Saber's face lit up when his children came alongside him. He said, looking down at them, "What do you say to the nice man who gave you candy?"

Both boys glanced up and said in unison, "Thank you, Mister."

"You're welcome." My voice sounded far away, like it was someone else's.

The Omega boy then took a step forward and reached up to touch my hand with his sticky fingers. "I had orange. It's my favorite. What's your favorite?"

I blinked down at him. His sugary Omega finger brushed my suit sleeve; it was only a two thousand dollar suit. I wasn't sure what to do. So I said the only thing that came to mind.

"Chocolate."

He grinned up at me, eyes beaming, face so open it almost hurt me to look at him. "I like that, too!"

Then, just as soon as he spoke, Saber ushered them out and, even as my office door swung shut, I could hear him talking softly to them as the little family padded down the hall.

I felt big and awkward and strange standing there listening to them leave, and then a rolling emptiness began to crawl up inside me.

Chapter Four

Saber

The image of the Alpha at the bank haunted me all day.

Mathias Vandergale.

Why did I keep thinking of him?

He was the son of one of the richest men in the country. What was he doing working at a bank and playing at being my guardian?

And what had I been thinking when I practically forced this Alpha to obey the rule to do a home inspection? He'd clearly given me an out and I didn't take it. What was wrong with me?

I wasn't so shallow as to be turned by a strong-lined face and broad shoulders. Though Mathias was big and dark complected—totally my type—I had more important things to focus on like my family and my pregnancy. Besides, he was too arrogant.

I could read him so well. He was the type of Alpha who thought he knew everything, and who had no time for lowly Omegas except to use them during his Burns. He'd actually suggested I send Tybor to an Omega chattel farm! The nerve! It was accepted practice by a lot of Alphas, but that didn't make it any less heartless.

Just before the kids' bedtime, Tybor came to me dressed in his pajamas. He'd become very independent lately, and insisted on dressing and undressing himself. His top was on inside out, but other than that he'd done a great job.

I sat on the couch with the TV on and he climbed onto my lap and put his arms around my neck. "Daddy." He put his mouth close to my ear and whispered. "You won't make me go away, will ya?"

My heart nearly stopped. I hugged him to me and said, "No, honey. Never. Why would you ever think it?"

"That man at the bank. The very very tall one."

I nodded.

"He said you don't have to keep me." He pulled back and I could see his face all scrunched up like he was trying to understand, while at the same time hold back his fear.

"I promise with all my heart, baby, I'm keeping you."

"Even after the new twins are borned?" he asked. "Maybe there will be too many of us?"

"Too many? How many do you think that is?" He was a whiz at counting for his age, bypassing Luke by far. And they hadn't yet started kindergarten.

Tybor held up his hand and counted on his stubby fingers. "Luke, me. One. Two. Then the new twins. That's one. And two." He held up four fingers and slowly counted them. "One. Two. Three. Four. Four kids. Four, is that right, Daddy?"

"That exactly right. Four kids. I have enough love to give to all of you. Love is one of those things that the more you feel it, the more you have. You never run out."

Tybor smiled. "I love you, Daddy."

"I love you, too, Tybor."

I scooted forward and picked him up in my arms as I stood. I felt a slight twinge in my back, but the pregnancy hadn't really taken much out of me yet. Even with twins, at over five months I wasn't showing all that much yet. I felt a heaviness down there and twinges in my lower back. Tybor and Luke had been a very easy pregnancy and I'd only gotten big in the last month before they were born. After they arrived, I'd recovered quickly, too.

"Let's go see to your brother and tuck you both in bed."

"Can't I stay up?"

"No, it's already five minutes past your real bedtime."

"Ugh." Tybor pouted.

When the boys were both put to bed with their teddies and their favorite blankies, I went back into the living room and tried to focus on the TV. But I kept thinking about Mathias.

Damn him for intruding. I didn't like the man at all. So why was this happening?

It would be an early day tomorrow, since the boys were always up by six or six-thirty, so I turned in early.

It was easy to fall to sleep. The boys were a full-time handful, and tired me out even though I was in prime health.

But as I slept, I kept waking with unnerving images of Mathias lingering in my mind. I tossed and turned all night, seeing his face, his long dark hair, and hearing his low voice tell me things. What those things were, I couldn't remember, but my restless thoughts and body seemed unable to let go of the feel of his presence.

I only dreamed like that when I was stressed. I never dreamed of Drayden, or any other Alpha for that matter. After Drayden died, I'd had a few nightmares about plane crashes, but that was to be expected. Mostly, my stresses were about family, my kids, and the fact that they were growing up so fast. They were already almost school age. I couldn't believe it.

Finally, with Mathias's face like an afterimage on my mind, I got up early, well before the boys, and made myself coffee.

I checked the accounts on the computer to see that all was in order. Mathias had sent me e-docs of the paperwork from yesterday, and I filed those away.

When I looked at everything online, I saw that Mathias had been true to his word. Nothing had changed. I had access to all my money. The only accounts that had daily limits were two savings accounts, one with money Drayden had frugally saved and left behind for me and the kids, and the other with the insurance money for his death. That was a large sum. My limits on those accounts had always been the same. $500 a day. They hadn't changed. Mathias had signed off on that as adequate, I guessed.

My other accounts were two checking accounts. One was for household stuff, mainly. The other was for extras, like vacations or things for the kids. There were no daily limits on those.

But as I scrutinized them, I saw that without more income, though they did earn interest, they would slowly dwindle over the years of raising my kids. I needed a job. Maybe not right away, and certainly not while I was pregnant and for a few months after when I had to take care of my new infants, but eventually.

The prospect terrified me. What kind of job could I hold? Menial, at best. A low level position that would help bring something in, but would never fatten my accounts.

I tried not to worry about it. For now we were fine, the boys and I. I didn't have to worry about this now, and technically not even for years to come. But I also was the responsible sort, and didn't like to think the future held nothing for me but a bleak, boring job and lonely days, especially after my boys were all grown.

I thought of Mathias again, with his severe but handsome features, and that long tight braid of black hair that gleamed down his back. He was a Vandergale. His father owned the bank that held my money. He'd never had to have a thought like this in his life. He wouldn't know what it was like. Unable to relate to me at all in that, here he was as my financial guardian.

I considered writing that letter I'd threatened to send yesterday, to formally request a new guardian. Mathias was simply all wrong for the job, I thought.

But I couldn't make myself open a blank screen on the computer to begin. Why would I want to go through all this again? Mathias obviously hadn't sabotaged me. He hadn't set limits, which he'd been in the right to do, and he'd seemed honestly convinced of my competence by my handling of my family's finances all along since before Drayden's death.

Still, I couldn't help but think Mathias didn't want the job, or anything to do with me, for that matter. Maybe it would be better to have someone who took an interest.

I knew Mathias's type. He saw Omegas as servants at the best of times, and at worst, holes to be filled during an Alpha's Burn. He no doubt did not approve of me raising two kids on my own, with two more on the way. I was a problem. Someone who didn't fit with his *society*.

I hated Alphas like that. Drayden had been one. He requested I be taken off my contraceptives for our dating, then knocked me up at the chattel farm and married me to be his nanny and maid. He had an image to keep up with his status at work and his friends. I was part of his brand, part of how he showed the world what a perfect Alpha he could be.

Drayden was never mean, but never warm, either. Mathias seemed much the same, so why couldn't I stop thinking about him?

I scratched my fingers through my hair and yanked. Ack! Was my mind stuck on him just because he was handsome? And he was, I couldn't deny it. Far better looking than Drayden, or any Alpha I'd known.

To distract myself from such thoughts, I checked on Tybor and Luke, who were both up and scrambling into their clothes, their shirts inside-out and half over their heads.

I helped them finish and they followed me to the kitchen where I turned on the TV while fixing them breakfast.

They laughed and played together, spilling more of their food than eating it, then ran off when they said they were full to set up their race car ramp in the living room.

"Hey," I said. "We're having a visitor. Can you set that toy up in your own room?"

They nodded simultaneously and scampered off together.

I looked at the clock. I had time to do some cleaning. First, the kitchen. When it was spotless, I turned to the living room before asking myself, yet again, what I was doing. Was I cleaning because Mathias was coming? What did I care how he saw me and my house? The expenses and finances were his expertise. He was coming to assess if I could afford to keep the place, and how I might make my money last.

Still, I got out the vacuum and began with the living room.

I piled up toys in a box.

I dusted.

I swept the front porch.

I even changed the sheets on the kids' beds and my own, and did two loads of laundry.

All the while I chastised myself that I'd lost my mind. But the house needed a good cleaning anyway. Drayden had liked me to keep things neat, but he was never home. I always left everything to the day before I knew he was returning for a few days off. This felt like the same thing. I was backtracking. Making my house neat for an Alpha I didn't even care for.

I hated every moment of it. The only thing I liked about being a stay-at-home dad was the kids. I loved them more than anything. But the chores sucked.

By the time I was satisfied enough with the house's appearance, I realized I had only five minutes to see to myself before Mathias arrived.

Hastily putting away all my cleaning tools, I started toward my room where I planned to change my out of sweaty shirt and comb my hair.

As I walked past the front room, I heard a knock.

Damn, he was early!

I pushed my hair back over my ears with both hands, straightened my t-shirt, and peered through the peephole.

I saw a big chest clad in a dark blue suit with a pink vest underneath and a darker pink tie with a solid gold bar fastened through the knot of the tie. Gods, he'd dressed up? My heart hammered in my chest before I realized he was simply wearing his work clothes. Yes, that was what he wore to work. Yesterday he'd been impeccably dressed as well for our meeting. Why would I have assumed otherwise?

Taking a deep breath to calm my stupid nerves, I put my hand on the door knob and opened it.

Mathias stood looking down at me, and one eyebrow rose.

I felt small and hot and sweaty. Ridiculously subservient. I knew better. I was smart, competent and definitely *not* inferior.

"You're early," I snapped. I almost cringed at the tone of my voice, but stepped back in a pretense of inviting him in.

"Am I?" he asked. He glanced at his gold watch. "Hmm, a minute or two," he said as if it shouldn't have mattered.

He was right, of course, it shouldn't have mattered. But I was feeling self-conscious. And stupid. This didn't have to be happening. I was the idiot who'd been too proud to give him his way and insisted he come by. I'd made the appointment, set the time.

Mathias. The Alpha son of Varian Vandergale. Big. Dark. Hair shining and perfect in a neat braid. Cuff links gleaming in the sunlight as he swung his hands forward, jacket sleeves riding up, and took his first step into my home.

I heard the tiny patter of footsteps behind me.

"Hey, I know you." The high pitched voice of Tybor spoke from behind my blue jeans clad legs. "Hi, bank guy."

Mathias looked down at him as Tybor came out from behind me. He towered over him—well, technically he towered over us all.

"You're the one who likes orange," Mathias said.

Tybor glanced up at me with wide eyes. "He members."

Luke came to stand beside Tybor. He had always been the quieter twin, shier, despite being the Alpha. He said nothing.

Mathias took two more steps inside, his hand going into his pocket. He pulled something out, then bent slightly at the waist and held out his hand. On it were two orange-wrapped candies.

"For us?" Tybor asked.

"Hmm, well, is there anyone else here who likes orange?" Mathias asked. He was so nonchalant about it all, so matter of fact. This rich man, this Vandergale.

What the hell was he doing here? What the hell was I thinking having made this appointment?

"Just me," Tybor answered excitedly.

"And me," said Luke softly.

"Well, then, I suppose they will go to waste if you don't take them."

Tybor's hand shot out and he grabbed one of the candies. Luke was slower, more deliberate.

"Daddy, can we eat them now?"

"You're ruining their lunch," I said with an exaggerated sigh, eyeing Mathias without turning away from my boys. Then I bent down to them and said, "Okay, you can have them. Now run along to your room and play while I show Mister Vandergale around."

"Yay!" Tybor and Luke leaped backward and ran down the hall, their sweet, excited voices echoing around us.

A silence fell between us.

Mathias glanced up at the ceiling, then around at the foyer that opened onto the living room.

I started to ask him to follow me, when he said, quite casually, "Bank guy?"

I blinked, startled. "Uh, he doesn't know your name. You never introduced yourself to him."

"No. I didn't." Mathias glanced at me, gaze holding mine for a little longer than felt comfortable, then his eyes dropped, grazing over my body all the way down to my feet.

"So," I said. "I guess we should make this as quick as possible."

His eyebrows rose.

"The tour."

"I can already see it's a very nice house."

"My Alpha took good care of us. But if it's too much for upkeep..." I let my words trail off. I really didn't want to have to move. The idea now, though, was to save as much as I could. Mathias was supposed to be the one to advise me.

"How many bedrooms?" he asked.

"Four. With two more kids on the way, I am going to need them all. Drayden used one for his office—my office now. Tybor and Luke sleep together. I have the master. But the fourth is the baby room. Right now it's more like storage, but I'm going to fix it up."

I was babbling like some insecure, pregnant teen. I knew it. But I couldn't stop.

We walked through the living room. It was large, furnished the way Drayden wanted it with two expensive leather couches and the biggest flat screen TV he could find. The floor was real wood. The tables were oak, the lamps all different, all handmade.

Mathias followed me through to the kitchen where black marble countertops shone with silver flecks. All my appliances were silver, including the fridge. I'd just cleaned everything so every surface gleamed.

Drayden had liked black and chrome, grays and whites. I threw in my own color when I could. I had a red teapot and red-handled cooking utensils in a silver metal vase by the stove. My stove top covers were multi-color abstract designs. I loved them.

But as I looked around at everything, a surge of adrenaline ran through my veins. Panic. Did it all look like too much? Was Mathias thinking I was somehow spoiled and should move down in class due to my circumstances?

The dining room beyond the kitchen was massive and overlooked plate glass windows showing off a view to my large backyard with its thick green lawns and flowerbeds. I had had help with the upkeep on it when Drayden was alive, but since his death, I was the one who kept things watered and mowed. It was fun because I got the twins to help out and they loved it.

But now I looked it all over and my every nerve went taut.

I didn't want to rely on Mathias's opinion, but in an Alpha ruled world, I had no choice. I stole a quick glance at him, but he seemed pretty relaxed, his face showing no indication of disapproval.

I took a deep breath.

"It's all one story. Let me show you the bedrooms. They are off the other side of the kitchen and down a hall."

The first bedroom was the office. It was done to Drayden's tastes, all black and white. The desk computer was on, flickering a pattern of a moving fractal. There was a huge white rug on the floor before the desk.

Drayden had not allowed the boys entry unless he was present and invited them. But now it was my office and my rules. My sons were allowed anywhere they wanted to go in the house. It was their home, too.

The next bedroom was the baby's room, dark with the curtains closed. I stored exercise equipment in there as well as the boy's baby things which would come in use for the new set of twins.

"I'm going to paint and stuff. I need new cribs because I sold the last ones. I'll need to budget for all that."

"Of course." Mathias still showed me no sign of his thoughts or opinions.

Next came Tybor and Luke's room. The boys were playing with a race track they'd gotten last Christmas. It was their favorite toy. They could build tracks in all different shapes and race their cars against each other as well.

Tybor and Luke looked up as we peeked in.

"Daddy, I'm getting hungry," Tybor said.

"Lunch will be in a few minutes, okay?" I replied.

"Okay."

My heart rammed against the walls of my chest as we moved on to the master bedroom. It felt weird, like this was an intrusion. The room was my private place, and yet I had only felt that way recently. It had been Drayden's room, kept how he liked it, and I'd always felt like the guest. Even after we bonded and married, I tiptoed around him.

Double doors opened onto the room. It was carpeted with black plush, which showed every speck of dirt and dust. Gray and black curtains framed wide windows that looked onto the side yard which had a big pine tree.

Normally, the spread on the bed was Drayden's choice, a black or white comforter, but I'd recently bought a dark purple one and used that. It was neatly made and I thought it made the room look more elegant than it ever had been when Drayden was alive.

The closet was a walk-in and the bathroom huge.

Refusing the guilt that tried to bubble up within me, I stood in the middle of the room, breathing a bit shallowly.

Mathias said nothing. He looked around once, then wandered back into the hallway. It surprised me that he had no tablet or notepad. He wasn't taking any notes.

I followed him back into the living room.

He turned and said, "Your home is perfect for raising a family with four children. With the housing market as it currently stands, if you moved anywhere else you would not necessarily save. Best to keep this place and the equity you already have. In time it will grow and the house's value will appreciate."

"But my mortgage is my highest bill."

"That's normal." Mathias said.

I didn't like that he was so quiet. "You're not saying much and it makes me nervous. I feel like there are things you're not saying. Opinions."

Mathias blinked and his long lashes flashed for a split second in the late morning light. "It just wasn't what I expected."

"What were you expecting?"

He looked down and blinked a little harder. "I don't know."

I didn't like feeling insecure about everything. When we'd met yesterday, I'd been upset about the hassles but had been entirely confident I could handle things. Now, Mathias and his casual manner had me questioning.

I was mad at myself for allowing him any power over me in that way.

"Well," I said, "if you can see a long-term outcome I can't, tell me. I don't like surprises and I have my kids to think about."

"No. You're fine. I can take a look at your home loan and see if I can find you something better with lower interest, but for now you have things handled."

"You weren't expecting that, then?"

He didn't answer.

I kept looking at his profile, and at his sleek hair, like a cat's, black and straight and impossibly shiny. I kept thinking about how broad he was, and yet trim at the waist, and how his suit jacket fit him so perfectly the tailor had to have measured him in every way possible—naked—to get it to fit every curve, every inch of him, the material pressing just right as he bent his arms, or as he stretched his shoulders back.

My skin heated to look at him, though I resented him in every way, his seeming uncaring expressions, his wealth, his intrusion into my home.

But I had invited him here. Realizing that made me grit my teeth as hot and cold tingles ran up and down my spine.

What was wrong with me? I became self-conscious in my old t-shirt and jeans, with my hair sliding forward over my forehead, not neat and tidy and pushed back like I preferred. I really had meant to shower and change before Mathias arrived. I'd mis-timed it and Mathias had been a bit early.

I wanted him to leave, but at the same time I wanted him to see that I was capable, that I was more than just an unfortunate pregnant Omega who'd lost his Alpha and couldn't take care of himself or his kids. That role was not me. Never had been.

Did I need to prove myself to him? Or to myself?

I blurted out before thinking, "We're about to have some lunch. Want some?"

What kind of invite was that?

I replayed my words and my tone over and over in my head. How rude I sounded. My cheeks warmed.

I gulped. "It's just sandwiches. Peanut butter for the kids. Cold cuts for myself."

Mathias tilted his head as if he were hearing an unfamiliar language.

"I mean, I know you're a busy man."

"Yes." But his tone dropped with that one word. His dark, sleek eyebrows came together.

What was I thinking? I didn't even know this Alpha. This Alpha who was technically the ruler of my funds. My body and mind simply weren't in sync.

My body wanted to move toward him, toward his height and broad shoulders, his prickly gaze, his utter nonchalance. It wanted to push through the barrier I could feel around him that was like dark glass waiting to shatter. It knew all of that which my mind rejected.

My mind told me Mathias was bored, put out, uninterested in the problems of lowly Omegas who should all be reared by other Omegas and live on chattel farms.

50

I should hate him or at the very least greatly resent him. He didn't see *me* when he made that remark about sending Tybor away. He saw in me a weak and helpless stranger who was good for only one thing. A hole for an Alpha's Burn.

My body wanted to preen. My mind wanted to rebel, ignore, snarl.

He stood staring down at me. He seemed to be waiting for me to say something more. He took a shallow breath and the insides of his lips glistened.

"What kinds of cold cuts?"

For a moment I heard only the buzz of the words. No meaning. My tongue pressed against my front teeth. "Uh." I blinked hard. "Ham. Roast beef. Salami."

He nodded briefly.

I could think of nothing more to do. I turned away from him and he followed me into the kitchen.

Chapter Five

Mathias

"Like this," Saber said. He folded the meat double and placed it on the bread.

I stood at the kitchen island looking at my own sandwich which was flat and looking lifeless. I didn't cook. I never made my own food.

The Omega should have been serving me, but the thought left me as soon as I glanced at his impeccable profile. Marble countertops and red name brand appliances meant his Alpha had bought the best. Or maybe it was Saber who had good taste.

He saw me glancing about the kitchen and said, "We just had the kitchen remodeled before Drayden died. Obviously, I won't always be so extravagant."

Extravagant? Father had raised his boys eating off imported China with fourteen carat gold forks and knives.

"You should have the best." I nearly coughed as the words seemed to fall from my mouth.

Saber gave me a hard look, but his eyes wandered back and forth as if assessing me over and over again.

Why couldn't I think right around this Omega? He was beautiful, but that shouldn't have mattered. I wasn't in the Burn, and when I was, I had tastes for the pretty ones, yes, like any Alpha, but mostly I didn't look at their full attributes, just their lower back halves.

We took our sandwiches and sodas to the table.

Luke and Tybor were already eating their peanut butter and jelly. Luke had a smear of grape jelly on his cheek.

"Napkin, Luke," Saber instructed.

Luke picked up his napkin and wiped his face, but the grape stain remained. Tybor was fastidiously neat, more focused. Luke was the Alpha. Yet somehow their personalities seemed opposite to their labels. But what did I know about Omega children?

Father had taught me well. Omegas were good for only one thing.

Admittedly, Father was an asshole. But his money was in endless supply, earned, deserved, privileged. How could I have wanted to emulate anyone else? He had everything he wanted: a mansion, servants, the finest Omegas when he needed them, people catering to his every whim, doting and pure Alpha sons. Except for Kris.

But no, Kris had been doting. The best of the best. Father's favorite, everyone knew. When Kris, the prize Alpha of our litter, had been diagnosed as an Omega at eighteen, though the parts inside him had been dormant since birth, atrophied, hidden, Father treated him as if he were diseased.

I didn't know how to feel, so I followed Father's footsteps. I believed something was wrong with Kris. And for some reason I believed he'd fooled us, keeping parts of himself hidden, keeping secrets. But he hadn't known. He couldn't have known.

I had blamed him for something he had no control over. I had behaved like the purebred Alpha brat Father had raised me to be. Now my litter-mate and brother, Kris, was a stranger to me.

In my life, I associated Omegas with the Burn, and therefore sex. That was all. Not a crime.

But Saber, this Omega, sat before me with his rumpled wheat-colored hair and firm eyes, his jeans and t-shirt fitting his form to show off his golden skin and lean muscles, and he was so much just a guy trying to raise two kids. A guy who was also pregnant.

A guy who'd asked me to stay for lunch.

Inside my chest, something lurched forward. The weirdest feeling swept over me, like he should be kept close, kept from all harm, treated like... like Father surrounded by his servants with all the best things, the catered foods, the luxurious rooms, the golden faucets on every sink and shower head, the furniture made to cushion bodies with the sweetest and softest of comforts.

Saber wasn't a stray I needed to bring home. He wasn't anything like that. He could take care of himself. Yet I responded as if he were in need, someone who should be protected.

I could feel the rise in me, a fierce craving, a heat-like arousal mixed with longing but disconnected from the blind force of the Burn itself.

To distract myself, I took a bite of my flat sandwich. I tasted little of it, chewing automatically, but had the impression it was the best sandwich I'd ever had because I'd put it together. It had been forward of me to reach for my own sandwich makings without Saber's permission, yet I hadn't been able to stomach the thought of having him serve me.

Why should he? I wasn't his Alpha. I was no one to him, and that idea prickled at the back of my mind. This wasn't my place. I didn't fit. Yet I wanted to see that Saber had everything he needed, that all the paperwork for his future was perfect, organized, and earning him the best interest.

More, I wanted to block him from any pain. His Alpha hadn't been nice to him? He deserved better. Did I think I was what he deserved? My body thought so, but my mind knew better. I was a prick. Like Father, I'd be alone forever. I'd chosen that road. And like Father, if I ever wanted children I'd hire an Omega to have them.

So far, I'd never wanted kids, but I looked at Tybor as he smiled at me, chewing a delicate bite of his sandwich which he held in both hands, and felt helpless.

I didn't smile back. Instead, I took more tasteless bites of my sandwich. I did not open the soda.

I knew I should leave. I didn't know these people and this little family was not mine and never would be. Obviously, my thoughts had gone haywire. I didn't hang with Omegas outside the Burn. Like father, like son.

54

Abruptly, I pulled out my cell pretending to check it, and stood. Half my sandwich lay uneaten on my plate. It was rude but this couldn't go on. I said, "I should be going now. I have meetings."

Saber scooted his chair back with a scraping sound. "Of course." He stood, looking down at the boys. "Finish your lunch." Looking up, he said, "I'll see you to the door."

"I can see my way out."

Saber said nothing, but accompanied me through the little hall and past the front room to the foyer. "I should have shown you the yard," he mumbled.

"No need. I saw it through your windows. Well kept." My skin heated. Too many times around this Omega, I wasn't thinking before I spoke. Would he take those last words as a sort of twisted criticism, thinking he should keep his yard nice because I thought so?

"Thank you," he replied. Simple. Not defensive.

"We should not need much further contact except by email if you have questions or there is anything else you need." Those words should have brought me relief. Instead, they made me more tense.

"Then I will email if I have questions."

Looking down at him, I had more odd thoughts. It was my day for them. I wanted to touch him. I wanted to lean down and smell his hair. Even now, at a distance of about one and a half feet, I scented him: Omega sweet as they all were, and the lilac fragrance I'd noticed yesterday, but with a hint of ionization around the edges, like a quickly put out match, or a distant fire. Salty, cloying, mouthwatering.

Saber was drawn taut, like me. We were the same in that way. But he didn't need me and I knew it. Besides, my conviction to be like Father, to remain alone, made the notion of being drawn to him preposterous.

He wasn't mine. I told myself that over and over as the front door closed behind me and I walked to my car.

He wasn't mine.

Chapter Six

Saber

In the night, I woke with the image of Mathias looming over me, his dark hair loose and floating all around him. Dreams. Just dreams.

They had begun the evening after our first meeting, and now ramped up this second night after the home inspection.

I tossed and turned in my big bed. I was used to sleeping alone. Drayden had been gone so much of our married life. But somehow, even though my day to day living hadn't changed all that much, things had begun to feel emptier, lonelier.

My pregnancy was going well. I had no morning sickness and only a little weight gain. That was normal. With Tybor and Luke I had not started to put on too many pounds or show until the third trimester. I had the musculature that held everything in place for a long time. In other words, said my doctor, I was the perfect healthy Omega standard for bearing young.

I sat up and turned on the light, reaching for a book. I couldn't concentrate. My skin was hot so I got up and turned on the shower. When I got in, the water pelted my skin until it was overly sensitive in a good way, and when I touched myself I came in moments. It felt wonderful. Except for the fact that Mathias's face and the memory of his scent accompanied the pleasure.

Lusting after my financial guardian? Honestly, it came as no surprise. He was handsome and big, the Alpha to a healthy Omega's fantasies. Why not? Except this Alpha was a Vandergale, completely out of my league.

My fantasies tended to be overwhelming like that. My first crush was on an Alpha I saw at the chattel farm who was already dating another Omega. I had other incidents like that, wanting what I could never have.

I turned off the water, stepped out of the shower and toweled myself dry. As I stood naked in the steam of the bathroom, I made myself ask the question out loud.

"Do you really want him?"

He had been cold, arrogant and standoffish. Yet he had backed off from completely controlling every angle of my finances. Though he'd made the comment about sending Tybor to a chattel farm, he had later shown my kids some semblance of respect.

I couldn't really tell if he liked kids or not, but Tybor had caught his attention. An Omega child. The type of child our society often overlooked. But Tybor had a personality everybody liked.

I crawled back into my bed, pulling the covers up tight over my naked body. I closed my eyes and immediately Mathias's dark visage was there in my mind.

Yes, of course I wanted him. But any chance I had was minimal. I had another Alpha's kids, which made me not the greatest catch in the world. Worse, I was pregnant. Plus, the lunch I'd offered him had been inadequate. He hadn't finished his sandwich. And he'd left too quickly afterward with the excuse of having appointments.

Now there was no reason for him to see me again. He was my financial guardian who promised to keep his distance, and that was that.

I pretty much resigned myself to being alone for the raising of my kids. I needed to get my mind off Mathias and focus on my family and my two children who were on the way.

Turning onto my side, I forced my mind to quiet. My body and my thoughts, however, had other ideas.

I tossed and turned. After a long time, when I finally managed to fall into a doze, there was Mathias waiting for me in my dreams with those sleek, narrowed eyebrows and a look that was made of barely held back impatience and condescension. He was probably an ass and a terrible lover anyway, thought my dream-self.

But my mind did not want to get rid of him.

Chapter Seven

Mathias

I sat at the long, sparkling table, Trigg at my side and Father seated, as always, at the head of the table. Our little brothers, Mica and Bren, sat facing us. Both boys were eighteen now and had already experienced their first Burns. Together, they were studying for their degrees in business and finance, never apart, even sharing the same dorm room at college.

They were on a break for a few days and had come home.

"It's nice to see my boys all together," Father said. "We don't get to do this often anymore. Cheers." Father held up his glass of three hundred dollar a bottle champagne.

Trigg grabbed his glass, as did Mica and Bren. I sat for a moment staring at my shining plate, seeing the dim reflection of myself in the surface: smug, hard, maybe even sinister since my eyes were always tightly drawn and my eyebrows pressed together.

Something didn't feel right tonight. I usually got along with Father, and my brothers were no problem. But tonight I was restless and uncomfortable. Not at all hungry, though the smells wafting in from the kitchen were wonderful.

The last food I'd eaten had been a sandwich. One I'd made myself from the cold cuts in Saber's fridge. I did not remember its flavor, or anything about it, really, except the company.

Saber.

I squirmed in my seat, the thought of his name and the image of the Omega's face in my mind making me feel too hot.

Suddenly, I realized everyone at the table was looking at me. They all had their glasses raised. I had not even touched mine.

"Mathias, are you not drinking for some reason tonight?" Father asked.

I didn't look at Father but slowly reached out to pick up my glass. The liquid swirled gold within.

"Kris should be here," I said softly.

I saw Bren and Mica's eyes widen and they glanced at each other. Trigg cleared his throat.

Father said, simply, "Why?"

I saw my own face tighten even more in the reflection of my plate. "Because he's our brother. And your son."

Father set his glass down hard. It made an odd thunk that echoed in the dining room and momentarily took away the glimmer and glamour of the dinner table.

"I think you understand the reasons why Kris isn't here."

"Yes. He's different. And he married your neighbor across the street, a marriage you didn't sanction."

"No more words need to be spoken of it."

I stole a glance at Father and saw his face had reddened a bit. There was more to the story than that. Father didn't want Kris around for other reasons as well. One of those reasons was that Father, in the confusion of a sudden early onset of his Burn, had tried to rape Kris.

What an Alpha did during his Burn was considered private, and if he broke the law, Alpha law was lenient. If you were truly considered a threat, you were labeled a dangerous Alpha and that went into official government records. Before any mate-bond marriage, that declaration had to be known by all parties upfront.

Father had never spoken of that night. Nor, to my knowledge, had ever apologized. Neither had I for my part in the drama. I'd blamed Kris and threatened him myself, seeing Kris as a threat to the way of life we'd always known in the mansion growing up. Kris was the outcast. Kris was the problem.

But I had only been eighteen at the time. I was thirty now, and the weight of my past deeds and my own unhappiness woke things inside me I'd never dealt with before.

I wanted to defy Father. Something I'd never dared in the past.

I swallowed hard, trying to keep my mouth shut but not succeeding. "I could walk across the street right now and invite him and his bond-mate to dinner. Then it would be complete. Our family."

Father's chest expanded. He stared at me so hard it felt like a crushing pressure. Finally, I looked up and directly met Father's eyes.

Father's face was like rock, his eyes volcanic. "You may be excused from this dinner."

I got up. I glanced at my brothers. The twins and Trigg were all staring at me, their mouths slightly parted, their eyes big.

I boldly met each gaze. There was no way I was going to show submissiveness tonight. To any of them, Father or my brothers. No way would I buckle. The repercussions might be extreme. Father could take things away from me, money, job… I had a lot to lose. But probably it would all blow over.

At least I owned my own house. If it came down to Father firing me, or freezing my huge trust fund, I could sell it. Plus I had my own savings from my exorbitant salary at the bank.

But surely Father wouldn't do anything so rash just because I'd brought up Kris. Kris was, after all, still Father's son, and my and Trigg's litter-mate.

I went immediately to the front entrance, ignoring the butler, Reilly, who held the door for me. I got into my car and sped away, though slowed when I came the short way, just down the lane, to Kris and Thorne's place.

It had been twelve years. I hadn't seen or contacted Kris in all that time. Once we'd been close. Trigg, Kris and I had done everything together growing up in that house. Nearly every moment of my childhood was with Kris and Trigg by my side. I had no memory of that time in my life without them both there.

As I drove by, I had to bypass the small hill that blocked the sweet, two story house where Kris lived. But when I could finally see it, a dark square against a moonlit sky, the windows glowed amber, as if all the warmth of the world had settled there, peaceful and comforting. I knew Kris and Thorne were very much in love. Bondmates. Married. Thorne had risked everything to take Kris from Father and keep him by his side.

I had always been envious of Kris growing up. He'd been smarter, the only blond in the family with a beauty that was called exotic, and then even before his first Burn, Kris had found true love.

Jealousy was a possessing demon of rage. That was what I had felt most of his life.

But now I didn't like that feeling. Not one bit. Not anymore.

As I drove slowly by Kris and Thorne's home, I thought again of Saber, of the lunch I hadn't tasted but was the best sandwich ever, of the Omega who certainly didn't need me but who had gotten under my skin nonetheless.

It was as if my mind filled up with the lilac-hot scent of Saber. I could almost feel him sitting next to me in the passenger seat.

Already, my mind went to work, figuring out a way that I could see the Omega again. It was ridiculous, really. My responses outside the Burn, my reactions to the guy's kids... I didn't want a family. I didn't want to marry.

But Saber would not leave my thoughts.

Chapter Eight

Saber

Tybor wailed and Luke kept trying to put his arms around him.

"Luke, leave him be," I said. "He has a time out."

Luke looked up at me with a worried stare.

"Come, Luke, come with me." I stood in the doorway of their bedroom and beckoned him out.

Luke followed me and I closed the door on Tybor's crying. Luke put his fingers in his mouth and hunched his shoulders.

"It's only for ten minutes," I told him. "We'll come back and get him when he's calmed down."

Luke nodded but said nothing. I knew ten minutes was an eternity to a child, so I put my hand on his head and petted his hair. "That's just a little while," I added.

I took him with me to the kitchen and sat him at the table with a coloring book and crayons while I started dinner.

Tybor had not done anything more than talk back to me and disobey when I told him to go wash his hands if he wanted to help me prepare dinner. I was tired of my day, and tired of high energetic boys who always wanted something. I snapped at him and he began to cry.

Of course I immediately regretted my harsh tones toward him, but I still had to put him in a time out. Those were the rules.

Sighing, I rubbed my hand over my face, pressing away my fatigue. Two nights in a row tossing and turning and two rambunctious boys had taken a lot out of me.

Just as I opened the freezer to see what I might fix for dinner, my cell went off.

I picked it up, not recognizing the number.

"Hello?"

Silence on the other line made me think it was a spam robot, until I heard breathing.

"Hello?" I said again.

"This is Mathias." A pause. "From the bank."

Mathias? "Uh, yeah. Hello. Is anything the matter?"

"I have a line on a home equity refi I'd like to talk over with you. It would save you a substantial amount of money in monthly payments."

Disappointed for a moment that he called about a mere loan, I kicked myself for the thought, then glanced at the clock. It was nearly five. The bank closed at five.

"Now?"

"Well, I have time now."

"But the bank closes in a few minutes."

"No, I meant I have time. I could, uh, meet you somewhere for dinner and we could discuss it. On me."

I leaned back against the fridge and opened my mouth to speak but no words came out. An Alpha was offering me dinner. But not just any Alpha. A rich and spoiled Alpha with the last name of Vandergale. An Alpha who barely cracked a twinge of a smile and showed little emotion toward me and my kids. The Alpha I'd been dreaming about for two nights.

I cleared my throat. "I've got the kids, though."

"Bring them. We'll meet wherever you want that has a kid's menu."

"Uh, okay. Then I guess how about Duprees. It's a diner off exit 29 on the 5."

"I'll find it. Half an hour, then?"

"I can do that."

I hung up. I glanced at Luke who had stopped his coloring and was staring at me.

"Are we going somewhere, Daddy?"

"Yep. I've decided we're going out to dinner tonight."

"Yay! Can I go tell Tybor?"

I took a deep breath and barely refrained from rolling my eyes. "Yeah, kiddo, go tell your brother to get ready. Don't forget your jackets. Both of you. Hear me?"

"Yes, Daddy!" Luke gave a whoop and ran off down the hall. "Tybor, Tybor," he called. "Your time out is over! We're going out to dinner!" I heard the door to his room open and their excited voices mingle.

My own body both tensed and heated at the thought of seeing Mathias again so soon. All the warning bells went off in my mind. No regular financial guardian offered to take a client to dinner. Not unless they had more invested in their proceedings than simple advice. Or there was something more between them than business.

The idea that Mathias might be interested in me had me hot and cold. I wanted to rebel. Show the system out there I could take care of myself. Yet, I wanted to see those dark eyes again, like distant space waiting for the light of a star. A challenge. I'd have to travel a long, long way to reach the source of life behind those guarded gazes of his. I loved a challenge.

But I'd made this mistake before, saying yes to a hardened Alpha thinking I could soften him, change him. Drayden could never quite be reached. Our mate-bond never fully formed though he'd dated me while I still lived on the chattel farm, then taken me away in a whirl. It had been what all my Omega friends and I had dreamed of together, to one day meet the handsome Alpha who would sweep us off our feet.

Drayden and I stayed together to make a family and after the boys were born, he was the provider and I was maid and nanny. And a convenient hole for his Burns. I was sorry it hadn't been more, yet I was happy I had my boys plus two more on the way.

Would Mathias simply be a repeat of my habit? My tastes ran to dark brooding Alphas with broad shoulders and maybe a grudge or two against life.

I needed to be careful there.

As I changed from jeans to suit slacks and a clean white shirt, I listened to the boys down the hall in their own room getting ready.

I went into the bathroom and forced my hair back from my face, spraying it to stay in place and not droop into my eyes. I hadn't had a haircut in a couple of months but it looked okay longer, made me feel younger.

For the second time that day I shaved, just to be sure. Many Omegas didn't shave at all, their body hair sparse even around their genitalia. I'd never been sparse, but I wasn't a bear, either. I didn't grow any hair on my chest. At least, not so far in my twenty-seven years.

I slapped on some aftershave before I realized what I was actually doing. Here. Right now. It was as if I were preparing for a date. Primping and preening for Mathias.

I froze, shocked at my behavior. The boys had me exhausted and I was pregnant. What was I thinking? I didn't need this added drama in my life.

Rolling my eyes at my own reflection, I swept from the bathroom and moved quickly down the hallway to the boys' room.

"Are you guys all set?" I asked, leaning in their doorway.

"Daddy, can I bring Teddy?" asked Luke, holding a fuzzy, stuffed brown bear.

"Not to dinner tonight, okay? I'll tell you what. Let's bring your coloring books and some crayons with us."

He dropped his bear on the floor, immediately distracted by the prospect of coloring. Luke loved drawing and coloring pictures. "Okay."

Tybor stared just past me into the hall. He kept his mouth in a thin line. He was still mad at me, I assumed.

"Come on, then. You got your jackets?" I could see they already had them on, but I always asked them for confirmation. It was the way they learned obedience and verification they had correctly done what they were asked.

"Yes," said Luke.

They each had matching sport jackets, Luke's blue, Tybor's red. Side by side, they looked absolutely adorable and there were some days I still couldn't believe they were mine, these two sweet boys.

Together we all traipsed to the front of the house. As we passed the kitchen I gathered their coloring supplies and put them in a tote.

When we arrived at the diner, the sun was setting, already gone behind the mountains to the west leaving streaks of bright pink and orange across the lower sky. The air smelled of car exhaust and grilling hamburgers. It blew cool against my hot face, but did nothing to cool the rest of my body.

Was this how I was going to be every time Mathias asked for some financial meeting me? I hoped not, for I already resented that I was required to have a financial guardian. My pride was a bit ramshackle and I didn't need to further damage it by playing into this crush, if that was what this was.

But as we walked through the front doors of the restaurant, my gaze didn't even need to scan the room. It landed instantly on Mathias sitting with his laptop open in a booth by a window. It was as if all my senses knew where he was without needing any more cues than his presence.

The host greeted us and said, "Table for three?"

"We're meeting him." I pointed in the direction of Mathias and as I did his head came up and he met my gaze and nodded. Dark-eyed, face neutral, the cheekbones and jaw firm, chiseled, the hair sleek and black against his scalp where it was always pulled back into a tight braid. He looked almost posturing. Intimidating. So my type.

The host let us pass.

As we arrived at the booth, I realized I hadn't thought through the seating arrangement. If we were going to conduct any business, I needed to face him. It would be easier. This put us in the position where one of my boys would need to sit next to Mathias.

"Should we get a table? Would that make this easier?" I asked, looking down at my kids.

Mathias glanced at them as if they were nothing. But then, in a supremely unexpected gesture, half his mouth quirked as if in the beginnings of a smile, and he reached alongside him on the seat and brought up two packages of coloring books and crayons. Each package had its own book and pack of crayons. One had a red cover, one blue. The clear cellophane sealing them was decorated with gold ribbon. He held out the red one to Tybor and the blue to Luke.

"For me?" Tybor asked. Those were the first words he'd spoken since his earlier time-out.

"For me?" Luke asked.

"Yes," said Mathias. He looked up at me. "Have a seat." He gestured across from me. "Tybor can sit next to me."

"Is that okay, Daddy?" Tybor asked.

My mouth had dried. "Uh, okay." I stammered my words.

I moved into the booth and sat with Luke beside me on the outside.

"Can I open it?" Luke asked.

"Yes." I nodded, looking from him to Tybor. Tybor's book showed pages of cars, all different, from fire engines to Ferraris. Luke's had sailboats and ocean liners.

The boys unwrapped their presents and immediately began to color.

"That was kind of you," I said softly, moving my tote bag with their other coloring supplies onto the floor by my feet.

I realized the gesture meant that Mathias had thought ahead, and had considered the fact of my boys tagging along for this meeting. He'd gone out of his way to buy them these gifts.

I wasn't sure what to make of it. Maybe he simply wanted them occupied, out of the way. Or maybe he actually felt something.

I didn't know. I didn't want to presume.

The waiter came by and took our drink orders.

"Milk for the boys, please."

Mathias looked at me. "Would you like some wine?"

Wow. I hadn't expected that. This was about some financial prospect for me, wasn't it?

"I can't. Pregnant, remember?"

"Of course," Mathias said. He looked at the waiter. "I'll have a glass. White. Sauvignon Blanc if you have it."

"Uh, we have a house white chardonnay," the waiter said, looking a little confused. It was a cheap diner, after all.

"That's fine," Mathias said, turning away as if he couldn't be bothered to waste his time over the matter.

"I'll have some water, please. And water for the boys in addition to the milk," I added.

"Daddy, can I have a cherry soda?"

"No, Tybor," I replied softly. "Not tonight. That's a special dessert treat, remember?"

The boys were already coloring, rapidly filling in blank spaces of shapes with bright greens, purples and reds, their attentions fixated. I had raised them to be polite and not too disturbing in public, but one never had guarantees with five year olds, let alone two of them.

I was used to the energy of just me and the boys. They were like a high pitched hum always running through my body, always present. But now the energy at the table included a rather glowering, heavier presence, unpredictable, impossible to ignore.

Mathias's attention was now on the open screen of his laptop, but his aura was almost visceral in the air about me. Beyond the high-end perfume of him, he had the scent of electricity zinging across open wires. Hot and sharp. Opening a craving inside of me I did not wish to admit.

I hadn't realized how mundane and routine my life had become until now, faced with this newness, having dinner with an Alpha who was still a stranger to me. It stirred things up. My mind and body craved the stimulus, surprising me.

For years I'd been fine with just the boys, and recently preparing for my later months in pregnancy. Maintaining a household cool and peace. Planning on chores such as getting the storage room ready for the babies, unpacking what baby things I could find in the garage of Tybor and Luke's that had not been sold or thrown out. Boxes of onesies. Two bassinets taken apart and stored against one wall. I had a list of things I needed: cribs for one thing, and new bedding for them, diapers, pacifiers, bottles. Little stuffed dogs, lambs, frogs. Rattles and teething rings. It was such a long list and I quite couldn't remember how I'd handled it all so smoothly the first time around.

It was overwhelming. Exhausting to think about. Almost boring when I should have been excited, or at the very least, somewhat enlivened.

Then enter: Mathias. I didn't want to think about how my feelings of loneliness surfaced pretty much from the moment I'd laid eyes on him.

Now he sat across from me, all dark and powerful like a storm on a horizon I could not take my eyes from.

Something inside now told me I'd been missing out, even before Drayden's death. For years now, I'd been pushing aside my adult feelings, burying myself in kids and home. Content. But nothing more.

No real excitement—in any adult way—had permeated me for a long, long time. Drayden's Burns had come the closest to offering that feeling, but in the erotic sense only. And with our mate-bond not being successful, I didn't feel the thrill I wanted or hoped to feel whenever he walked into a room, or whenever I looked into his eyes.

Mathias glanced up at me. "I understand you are six years into a thirty year mortgage."

70

A fire started in my abdomen. No, I wasn't turned on by mortgages. But yes, I was sort of falling into his voice.

He was getting straight to business, and from him I expected no less.

"That sounds right," I said, working to keep my voice even.

"I can get you a loan at two percent. Yes, it will start over for thirty years, but your mortgage payments would be down by thirty percent. A significant savings."

"Oh, wow. How did you find that loan?"

Mathias raised his eyebrows as if offended. "It's what I do."

"Mortgage loans?"

"No. I find the best investments for my clients at the best rates."

"I'm not investing."

"No, but I am your financial guardian, so I figured--" He stopped and sat back as if caught at something he shouldn't have been doing. He swallowed and I watched his Adam's apple rise and fall. "I'm simply informing you of a good opportunity. No strings."

Stop questioning him, I chastised myself. "Well hell yeah I'm interested. I've got two more kids on the way. That money can go toward them."

Mathias got a look on his face that might have been admonishment, like of course I should say yes to this offer. Of course he was right about this. But his mouth relaxed and his eyes softened.

"Exactly what I was thinking," he said. He glanced at Luke and Tybor, who were coloring and quietly talking to each other in their shorthand twin language.

I felt a strange pang. Was this Alpha really concerned about the welfare of my children? Or was this him just doing his job?

Mathias continued to regale me with the benefits of the refi with his rich, smooth-gold voice, and everything sounded great, though I didn't hear many of the words. I kept being cajoled by his tone, and the strangely alluring idea that maybe he, Mathias Vandergale, really wanted what was best for me. He was a man who could do anything, have anybody. Financial guardianship wasn't even his real job. He'd been filling in for someone else the day I'd arrived for our first meeting.

I realized he'd finished his spiel and was waiting for my response.

"Sounds good," I said. "So you really have my best interests at heart?"

His frown caused a deep wrinkle between his eyebrows. "Why would you think otherwise?"

I shrugged, pretending I had nothing to lose. Playing cool. "I don't know. People get hoodwinked all the time on bad loans."

"Hoodwinked?"

"Yeah."

"Why would I do that to you? I don't need your money."

"How do I know how the Vandergales got so rich in the first place?"

When I said those words, I realized I might have gone too far. Not only had I insulted his efforts to put me in a better financial position, I'd insulted his name. And the bank he, or rather, his father owned.

I opened my mouth to try to take back my words, apologize, but before I could say anything, he started to laugh.

"Oh no," he said between chuckles, though still his lips did not smile. "You have it all wrong. We only hoodwink our competitors, and our enemies. You are neither."

"And what am I?"

He leaned back and folded his arms across his chest. "You're someone who has a substantial amount of money at our establishment. And we'd like to keep it that way."

"Oh." He'd said *someone*. Not Omega, but *someone*. I'd gained a few steps with him, then?

I picked up my water and took a sip. "So," I said. "Does that mean I should trust you?"

His eyelids half closed and he paused for a moment longer than was quite comfortable for business proceedings. His nostrils flared slightly. "The question is not should you, but can you," he finally replied.

"All right then." I'd play. "*Can* I trust you?"

One sleek eyebrow rose. "Most certainly."

At his words, my insides gave a little tremble. That was when I realized fully this was about more than a mortgage refi.

It was ridiculous. Me and him. Really, it was. I was nobody. He was a Vandergale. But my instincts came with clarity enough to see he was attracted in some way to me. Perhaps not as much as I was attracted to him. Which was maybe why he'd found this new loan for me. He didn't have the balls to ask me out, but he did have the know-how to find me a great loan.

"All right, then," I said. "Let's go for it."

He looked at me questioningly, as if he, too, had been lost in his thoughts.

"The loan," I said. "It sounds wonderful."

"It is."

The rest of the meal was shop talk, but the boys didn't seem to mind, and I was happy to be getting a good deal and to have better insight into this Alpha who had gone out of his way for me when he didn't have to.

We ended the meal with him promising to bring me the final documents to sign, which we would go over together.

To test these new waters, I asked, "Can't you email them with explanations?"

He took a deep breath. "It's best to go over it in person."

I nodded. Hiding my smile. "How soon can this be done?"

"The funds are available and you qualify. I just need to have the bank's loan officer draw up a few more papers for me."

"I was approved that quickly?"

"Well, when I put it through myself, with my name attached, yes."

Of course he'd seen to all that already, as if he knew I'd say yes. "All right. Whenever you say, then."

"Tomorrow."

"Tomorrow?"

He nodded as if this weren't out of the ordinary at all. But I knew this was not standard procedure for loans. *Mathias. What is going on in your mind?*

"I can be at your office any time."

"I can come to your house so you don't have to make the trip with your children."

Bold. Forward. Also considerate. I secretly liked it. "That's fine, too."

"All right then. How about two o'clock?"

"Hmm." I wadded my napkin in my lap and held it tight. "I owe you a dinner. How about five? I'll cook."

Maybe I was too forward and bold myself. Maybe he wouldn't like that in an Omega he was eyeballing. I waited with my breath held for his response.

"I will be there," was all he said.

His words left me wondering again, but then I remembered how quickly he'd found this loan and pushed it through for me, needing only my approval and signatures to finalize it. Who did that in this day and age for a stranger?

Yeah, Mathias was into me. Even if it was just for a single fun time, I was looking forward to it.

Chapter Nine

Mathias

From the side of my Ferrari a few parking spaces away, I watched Saber fuss over putting his kids in the backseat of his car, then get into the driver's seat and glide off. A strange sensation came over me. I wanted to follow him. Letting him out of my sight seemed wrong.

In my gut a kind fluttering began, as if something at dinner hadn't settled right.

The evening was still young but I felt exhausted. I shouldn't have been so tired, but the night before I'd slept little, waking often with dreams still hovering, blurred, meaningless, forgotten.

But I knew what they were about. My body understood. My attraction to Saber flared. I wanted. I wanted what I couldn't have.

Did Saber feel it? Sometimes when he looked at me with his clear blue eyes as if I were the most confounding being he'd ever met, I thought maybe there was something there behind the competent, no-fucking-around image, behind the sweet Dad he was with his kids. Something fiercely longing. Something that wanted more. It was why he'd not balked when I'd offered to come over to his house with more paperwork. Why he'd invited me to dinner instead of just a meeting during the afternoon.

I was terrible at reading people. Maybe I never tried hard enough.

Growing up, I had always known what Kris and Trigg were thinking, or what made them tick, but that was different. They were my litter-mates.

But after my dinner with Saber, I had a new outlook on my stunted abilities at seeing any motivations deeper than financial greed or a desire to get ahead in life.

The people I hung out with were easy to read. They wanted fun and wealth. They wanted long vacations, the best attire, and great sex. Some of them attained all of it. Most did not. But they really never looked beyond their own greed.

Saber was different. For one thing, he had kids, so of course he would be looking out for their welfare before his own needs. But there was much more to him than that. His kids made him strong, fierce, even, but within him glowed an intelligence and force I'd not really seen or thought about Omegas having.

In truth, I hadn't bothered to look. Father's lessons hooked deep. Omegas were good for cooling the Burn and bearing young. That was it. Father's cold pronouncements had easy access into my being since even as a kid I was always looking for the easy way out, the way to get what I wanted without much thought, and zero responsibility to whatever party had what I needed.

It was easy for me to handle my Burns while defining Omegas as necessary tools ready and waiting for me. It kept me from having to think.

When I first discovered that other Alphas often knotted during their Burns—all my friends did, and Trigg as well—I thought something was wrong with me because I never knotted. It never happened.

I didn't like that maybe I was different. Like my brother Kris was different. In my daily thoughts, I often blamed my Omega partners for my inability to knot. They weren't into me. They didn't mesh with my way of fucking. Or perhaps they actually hated me.

If I didn't care, I didn't have to worry. I didn't need to knot to get off and handle my Burns. My virility was fine—Father had us checked in every way by a doctor before we all turned eighteen.

I closed myself off. I didn't like the idea of marriage or family, so I refused to date. If I ever wanted to pass on my own legacy, I'd do as Father did. I'd buy an Omega breeder and have him carry my children. I'd keep the Alphas and discard the Omegas to farms. What was good enough for Father was good enough for me.

Sometimes I fucked Omegas outside the Burn, but mostly when I was younger, and at friendly parties where the Alpha hosts supplied them—rented from brothels or a nearby farm—and we all got drunk before, during and after. I never hosted parties like that myself. But yes, I fucked a hole when it was available.

Such parties were annoying when the fucking was public, though. A lot of the attendees would knot the Omega they were claiming, and sometimes there weren't enough Omegas to go around. Drunk, I'd sit on a couch or chair and watch while the Alphas yelled in ecstasy that seemed to never end.

I didn't like doing it at all, because maybe the other Alphas would see that I never knotted and begin to question me.

I liked my trysts in private rooms. I liked to come and go. Have it over with fast.

Things went along fine for me. I partied. I took long vacations with other rich Alphas, and I indulged in the finest of everything. To keep my shape, I had strict workout rules for myself. The routines kept me fit while I watched my Alpha equals develop pot bellies and even questionable hygiene.

In that regard, Father also raised me to be the best I could be, which meant daily bathing and impeccable clothing. It meant tidy, neat, every hair in place.

Alphas sometimes propositioned other Alphas. I had had a few offers. I declined. Most were intimidated by me.

Trigg once said, "You have a hard stare and people who want to feel good are turned off by that."

"Fuck off," I'd replied.

"You made my point." But he'd laughed because he knew growing up I was the snarky one, that I loved to intimidate and joke around about power plays and all the Omegas we would one day be having our way with. I used to be the funny one, the life of the party.

What had happened? I'd gotten jaded. Tired, I guess.

Until Saber.

I'd never met an Omega like him before. I'd only met the ones at the farms, brothels or those few I'd seen around the bank who were already mate-bonded and therefore off limits, nothing to me anyway.

When I got home, I went straight to my home office and quickly finished up and printed out the paperwork I would need tomorrow for Saber. Putting it into its own folder, I neatly stacked it beside my computer.

I'd told Saber it had been no big deal, that this was part of the job. But I'd lied. This loan had taken me the better part of the day, which was why I'd called last minute to invite him to dinner. And tonight I'd just killed over two hours, complete with emails and late hour phone calls to those assisting me, to get it completed. I could tell they were pissed or put out, but they didn't dare argue with me, and all delivered what I wanted within a short time.

It was no small task. I'd done this loan all right and proper, no cutting corners. I declined the commission as well, which meant Saber had gotten an even better deal than I'd promised him.

Now I checked my private messages. There were six from Trigg. I'd been ignoring him all day.

He'd sent a variety of texts.

Hey, Math. What the fuck is with you leaving me to fend for myself at Father's dinner?

Hey, are you ignoring me?

Math, what's going on with you?

If you want to know what happened after Father made you leave last night, well, nothing. Father refused to speak on any subject concerning you.

It's been a full day. Are you ignoring my texts? I wish I could have followed you out, but no use having Father on both our asses at the same time, right? I want to know, though, what made you bring up Kris? You hate it when I bring up his name in conversation. So what's up?

I'm up late tonight if you want to talk.

I pressed the call icon to Trigg on my computer. The screen gonged with his immediate response and his face appeared before me.

Trigg made a surprised face. "Bro, it's you. You finally got my messages?"

"Obviously. You are persistent."

"Are you okay? I mean you and Father usually get along. I don't remember you ever being dismissed from the dinner table except maybe when we were kids."

"I'm fine."

"Have you talked to Father at all?"

"No."

"Well, that's not like you. Something's going on in that beady swollen head of yours."

I sighed. "Yeah? Something's going on?"

"I know you too well, Math. What is it, something at the bank? Something else? You haven't been quite right since your last Burn."

"What? What do you know about it?" I shut my mouth hard. There I was giving myself away by being defensive. Trigg was not going to let up now.

"I'm just saying I notice, that's all. Like you were when Kris left. For a long time you didn't even speak to *me*."

I glared at the screen.

He put his hands up in a mea culpa gesture. "I know everything changed for us back then. All of it. The dynamics of the household. College. Everything. It was a harder time for everyone, okay?"

What could I say to him? I wasn't going to go backwards now and talk about all this. I remembered my fury. After twelve years, there was less fury. Maybe even regret. I gritted my teeth.

"I don't want to talk about that time. I hated Kris, okay? But maybe now I don't so much. I was a stupid kid." In many ways, I still was. If I were to be honest, I didn't really like myself after what had gone on with Kris, and after Father chose me as his second favorite. It dug a deep wound. *Second best.* I hated it. Trigg never cared about that stuff, but he'd never been competitive like I was. I was so damned competitive I'd cheat to get ahead.

So now what did that make me at thirty, working for Father in a name position only, living in luxury I barely earned, not to mention being an Alpha who couldn't knot?

I was a failure and that was that.

My last Burn had pissed me off. I'd felt so little with the Omega who serviced me and I wanted more.

Well, I always wanted more. I was a brat prick that way.

I heard Trigg say softly, "I just wish you'd talk to me."

"I am talking to you. This is what's called talking."

"Yeah," he said. "I can see your mouth moving, but I don't hear it saying a damn thing."

I pressed my palm to my forehead. Some of my hair came away from my severe hairstyle—the braid—and wisped across my temple.

"Maybe we need a vacation from all this," Trigg suggested when I didn't say anything.

It wasn't the locale that made me miserable. But I shrugged. "Where to this time?"

80

"Skiing or swimming? Fishing or hang gliding?"
I said nothing.

"White water rafting? Meditation seminar?
Monastery with a vow of silence? Science fiction
convention?"

"I'll think about it," I said. But all I could really
think about was the dinner tomorrow at Saber's house. I
wondered what he might cook. I wondered if he was
thinking about it, too.

"I wish you would tell me what's on your mind,"
Trigg said.

"I guess I'm just tired."

"Acting like an old man already?" Trigg snickered.

"Yeah, well, time flies, right?"

"Dude, don't be a stranger, okay."

I nodded.

"Text you tomorrow," he said.

"I'm sure you will," I replied.

He cut the line.

Chapter Ten

Saber

"You boys must be on your best behavior," I said, brushing Tybor's pale hair from his eyes. "Mister Vandergale is coming over again today and he has some very important papers for me."

"Daddy, is that man helping us?" asked Tybor.

"Yes, he is."

"Good. He's very big and tall and sometimes he looks mean, but he's not. I can tell. I like him."

"I miss Father," Luke said softly.

"I know." I brought him into a hug against my thigh. Drayden had been *Father* and I was *Daddy*. It had always been that way.

"Okay," I said, rubbing my hands together. "It's going to be steaks on the grill tonight for me and Mister Vandergale, and for you boys, you get a choice. Hamburger or hotdog."

"Hotdog!" said Luke.

"Hamburger!" said Tybor. "With ketchup."

I laughed. "One each coming up."

I had gone shopping earlier, and had everything I needed for a good dinner. The potatoes were already baking in the oven.

I brought the boys with me into the kitchen where they sat at the island on stools. They wanted to color in the books Mathias had given them in the diner.

While they created art, I made a tossed salad. I kept glancing at the stove clock, counting the minutes until Mathias's arrival.

The baking potatoes gave off a mouth-watering aroma. I had rolls in a package but decided it was too much. The food I had already prepared would be enough.

The steaks were seasoned and waiting for the grill which I would light when Mathias arrived. The hamburger patty and hot dog for Tybor and Luke were ready to go on the grill as well, and each one had its properly designated bun. I'd bought a pre-made apple pie for dessert.

The doorbell rang.

Both boys started to climb down from their stools.

"You guys stay right there," I told them. "I'll get it."

Tybor pouted but they both obeyed and went back to their coloring.

When I opened the door I saw Mathias standing with his hands full of bags and an attaché case under his arm.

If he had looked amazing last night, he was even more handsome tonight. The whites of his eyes were like gleaming lights surrounding beautiful, dark irises. He wore no tie, which made the pale blue dress shirt go into a V at his neck and showed off his gorgeous dark skin tones. Over that shirt, he wore a light gray blazer with matching trousers. The blackness of his braid glimmered against those paler colors, resting over his right shoulder.

I reached out and took two of the bags from him. "I told you I was cooking. What is all this?"

"Hmm. I was taught never to go to anyone's home with my hands empty."

"You're bringing me a refi that will save me a fortune. I think that's quite enough."

I led us into the kitchen area.

The boys looked up and in unison said, "Hi."

"Hello," Mathias said. Then he peered down at Tybor's book. "A purple fire engine?"

"Purple is my favorite color," Tybor said proudly.

"Mine, too," said Mathias, and set his goods next to them on the counter.

I saw one of the packages was a wine bag.

"I told you I can't have any of that." Without thinking, I placed my palm over my abdomen.

Mathias put his hand over the top of the bag. "It's cider."

"Oh." A warmth suffused through me that he'd cared that much. "Great."

As Mathias began taking things out of the bags, I saw that it was too much. Cookies. Fruit salad. A platter with crackers, meats and cheeses.

"We aren't going to be able to eat all that," I said.

"I know," he replied as if it didn't matter. "Hey," he said, digging to the bottom of the bag. "What's this?"

"What?" asked Tybor.

Luke looked up from his drawing.

Mathias pulled two little stuffed toy kittens from the bottom of the bag. They had big golden eyes. One was purple, the other blue.

The boys' mouths dropped open.

"I wasn't sure if maybe you two are too old for these, but I liked them. Who ever saw a purple or blue cat?" he asked.

"Maybe in cartoons?" said Tybor helpfully.

"Do they have names?" Luke asked.

"I thought maybe you could name them," Mathias replied. He looked at Tybor. "You said purple is your favorite color, right?"

He nodded, mouth still wide open.

Mathias handed him the purple kitten.

Luke said, "I love blue!"

Mathias handed him the blue kitten.

Both boys instantly snuggled the soft-furred toys into their shining, smiling faces.

"What do you say to Mister Vandergale?" I asked them.

"Thank you, Mister Vannerga." They did their best to pronounce his last name correctly. Well, we'd work on that.

I picked up the plate of meat and motioned out the sliding glass doors with my head. "Want to join me at the grill?"

84

"Of course." Mathias walked with me and opened the doors for me.

"You didn't have to bring them more presents," I said.

"I know. I'm not trying to be the cool uncle or anything," he replied.

"Aren't you?"

The boys followed us outside, running out onto the grass toward their swing set, their kittens hugged tightly in their arms. I turned on the grill and watched them put their kitties on swings and try to give them a ride. Of course the plush toys fell immediately into the dirt.

"I knew those toys weren't going to stay new and clean for long," I said.

"Machine washable," Mathias replied calmly. "I checked the tags."

I turned on the propane grill and started placing the meat over the flames. "Do you like your steak rare, medium or well-done?"

"Rare," he replied, watching as the kids zoomed around their swing set, their kitties held high as if they were making them fly.

"So," I said, trying to fill the empty silence between us. "I figure we can eat first, do business later. The kids are hungry and, well, so am I."

"Good. I came with an appetite."

The way he said it—*appetite*--sent a tingle down my spine. It was stupid. I didn't need any type of hook up or relationship right now. Honestly. And what would the neighbors say so soon after Drayden's death?

I didn't know what I could be thinking, allowing these feelings to surface.

As the steaks sizzled on the grill, the scent of charring beef made my mouth water. But more, the tall presence at my side filled up an emptiness I'd been feeling for too long. I suddenly had many hungers all at once for good food, friendship, and more.

But I didn't need an Alpha to take care of me and my family. I could handle it. I wasn't some poor swooning little Omega, and had never thought of myself that way.

Yet this moment felt like one to cherish. I watched my children play along the green grass, turned the steaks on the grill, flipped the burger and hot dog. I felt the heartbeat of a man by my side that lent me peace, strength and wholeness.

What was happening here?

In no time the food was done. I forked the meat onto a big platter and called the boys.

"It looks perfect," Mathias said.

I smiled to myself at the compliment.

In the kitchen, I took the potatoes out of the oven with my mitts. Then split one between the boys and dropped the other two on two plates.

"Everything's ready."

The boys took their places at the dining room table facing each other. That left the two ends, one for me, one for Mathias.

I got out the wine glasses for the cider and poured the boys their milk.

Without asking, Mathias picked up the salad dish and brought it to the table, then came back and helped me with all the plates and glasses.

"Can I have ketchup?" Tybor asked when I put his burger in front of him.

"Me, too," said Luke, never to be outdone.

When I finally sat, I saw Mathias helping the boys by serving a salad portion onto their plates. I wondered what he was thinking. Technically, yes, he'd brought documents for me to sign. And technically, yes, I'd invited him to dinner. My idea. But he was inserting himself here in a casual manner that let me know that this was more than a business meeting.

Both boys had set their toy kitties on the floor at their feet. It was clear they adored their gifts. But I still wasn't sure. Was this interest fleeting? A one-off for an intrigued Alpha? Or did Mathias want more?

I decided I'd be all right with whatever happened. It was a decision I'd made when I found myself primping for the dinner last night. I was in. I wanted this. I hoped he wanted this—whatever it was—too.

No one was speaking. Everyone had their mouths stuffed full of good, hot fresh food.

After taking a sip of the cider, which was wonderful, I asked, "What do you like to do when you're not working at the bank all the time?"

Mathias gulped. "I run in the mornings. I work out four times a week at night. Take vacations. Hang out. The other night I had dinner at my father's." He glanced down as if he hadn't meant to say that last part.

"Do you see your father a lot?" I asked.

"No."

"Why not?" Tybor piped up.

Mathias grazed him with a dark look. Tybor looked at me with his mouth scrunched up, as if he'd said something wrong.

Mathias said, "Sometimes my father isn't as nice as yours."

"Oh." Tybor blinked, thinking about that. "My daddy is nice."

Mathias winked at him, breaking the tension. "I think you're right."

My heart fluttered in my chest. I wondered what Mathias was alluding to by saying he didn't see his father often. Obviously he worked for him. I had many questions, but now wasn't the time.

The kids ate most of their hot dog and burger, then picked at their potato halves and salads.

Mathias had a great appetite, though, and cleaned his plate quickly. At last I had been able to offer him a meal that was more than a lousy sandwich.

At five months pregnant, I got hungrier more often, but I couldn't eat huge meals in one sitting. I saved half my steak, ate most of my salad and potato, and realized I had no room for pie.

"Maybe we can wait on the pie until a little later," I suggested to the table.

That was me presuming Mathias was even going to stay later than he had to after I signed the documents he'd brought.

Tybor and Luke wiggled in their chairs, waiting to be allowed to be excused.

"Can we watch a movie?" Luke asked.

"Yeah. Go ahead, guys. You may be excused."

They grabbed their stuffed kittens and ran off to the living room shouting, "I get to pick first!"

"No, I get to!"

I got up to clear the table. Mathias said, "I'll help."

I didn't really want Mathias's help. It seemed too personal, somehow. Yet he'd already inserted himself here by bringing groceries and giving my kids gifts. Careful, I told myself. Don't read too much into this. If he wanted more from me, great, but if he didn't, I had to be all right with that, too.

"All right, then."

We made a good team, rinsing and stacking the dishes in the dishwasher. It felt both odd and right.

After the dining table was cleared and with the dishwasher running, we sat there with me facing the living room down a short, wide hall so I could keep an eye on the kids.

Mathias opened his sleek attaché case and pulled out his laptop and a paper folder. When he had everything set up, he said, "It's fairly straightforward. Just need some signatures."

He slid a document across the table to me.

I saw the figure for the new payments right away. "Is this right?"

I pointed at it.

He nodded. "I'm not taking a commission so it's a slightly different number."

88

It cut off another hundred dollars in the monthly payment. "Shouldn't you take a commission? Isn't that standard?"

"There are still commissions. The loan officer I used gets one."

"I was talking about you."

"I'm fine."

But it felt like taking charity. He'd already found this loan, bought us dinner, given my kids things. Sure, those weren't exorbitant things, but I couldn't help the pang of guilt that washed through me.

I pushed the paperwork back toward him. "You should redo the numbers then. I want you to have a commission."

"I get paid by the bank quite handsomely. I'm not a loan officer and this procurement is part of the guardianship. The bank is taking a fee for that."

"Oh." I hadn't thought of that even though to begin with it had pissed me off. Financial guardians were not provided for free.

I might often feel screwed just for being an Omega, but suddenly I realized Mathias wasn't going to screw me over just because I was one. A warm rush of affection for the stoic Vandergale Alpha came over me.

I took back the paper. He'd highlighted in yellow marker where I was to sign.

It took us about ten minutes to get everything completed.

"Well, that was pretty easy. Don't these types of things take longer to go through the system?"

Mathias arranged the papers into the folder and closed it. "Not if it's approved right away. And it was."

I wasn't sure I believed him.

He put the folder into the attaché case and shut the lid on his computer.

There was nothing else for us to do but I didn't want him to leave just yet. I thought quickly. "You can't go yet. There's still apple pie."

I was grasping, I knew. When Drayden was dating me—the chattel farm called it *courting*—he would pick me up and take me out to dinner, then back to his place for an evening of fun. We'd have drinks, watch a movie, and always he wanted to have sex.

It was different for me now. I had kids. And Mathias? I couldn't tell if he'd ever dated in his life.

Alphas who stayed single for any length of time were usually the sort who weren't ready for families, drowning in their careers, or they were queer for Alpha/Alpha relationships. Mathias seemed the type who took what he wanted, so if he'd wanted an Omega or a relationship, he'd have had it.

Maybe he was like me and had lost someone?

I hadn't done this in so long I was wary of breaking the ice with him.

I decided to start with the subject of kids, since it was right there in front of us, the TV in the living room blaring some cartoon.

"So I take it you haven't been around kids too much? Not that you haven't treated my two like gold."

"My twin brothers were their age when I turned eighteen. I am thirteen years older."

"Identical?"

"Yes. But both Alphas."

"That's the usual with identicals. Tybor and Luke are more rare. If you get an Alpha and an Omega in twins, they're usually fraternal. It's about one in every ten thousand identical twin births that will result in one of them developing internal Omega organs."

"You've done your research."

"I wanted to know all I could about my boys."

"They are mirror twins."

"Yes," I replied, happy to hear he knew what that was. "Your brothers… are you close?"

Mathias turned his head as if to dismiss me. But I had begun to learn his mannerisms and I could tell he was actually thinking through his response. This communicated to me he had something to hide.

"Bren and Mica are the twins. I see them on holidays. I'm part of a triplet litter. We're all different. I keep in touch with Trigg, the third-born."

"And the other?"

He placed his hand, palm down, on the wooden table and his fingers started to rub the hard surface. "No. But I've been thinking about, uh, contacting him. I don't know."

"You don't have to talk about it if you don't want." I got up, grabbed the cider, and poured us each another glass. "I was just asking."

Mathias shrugged, eyebrows going up. "I rather fucked things up with him, I think. It's in the past."

But it wasn't in the past if they still weren't speaking. I kept my mouth shut.

Now Mathias turned his gaze on me, dark and unreadable. He took a deep breath, let it out slowly. He started to speak, then closed his mouth.

"What is it?" I asked. "If nothing else, after all you've done for me, I can at least return the favor by listening. I've been told I'm a good listener."

"You have kids. Listening is a skill you exercise, I'm sure." His lips quirked up a little.

"Gods, yes. Those two? Sometimes I can't get them to shut up." I laughed.

Something was going on between us. I could feel it—had been feeling it for a couple days. Clearly, it made Mathias uncomfortable. But he showed me he felt it, too, by not rushing off. By bringing my kids toys.

"You should know up front," he began. He swallowed hard. "Because I'm your financial guardian now."

"Know what?"

"I'm not really the good guy."

I sat back and crossed my fingers over my small, but no longer flat belly. "Oh?"

He was immaculate in his appearance, sharp-featured, expensively doffed in a lingering scent of fire. He was a calculating man. I'd already assessed that.

"I'm just not sure who I am anymore."

"Have you been questioning things for a long time?" I asked.

"Not really," he replied.

"Hmm." I tapped my fingertips on my belly. "Well, I don't really know you well. My first impression of you was sort of off. But from what I've seen, everything you've done for me and my kids in just a few days, it's, well, it's a good guy type of behavior."

One eyebrow rose in his habitual fashion. "It's not that I don't know how."

"Huh. Well, Tybor really likes you and he's a pretty good judge of character for his age."

"Is he?" Mathias asked.

Unspoken was the question, *What about you?*

Mathias rubbed harder at the table. "I would like to apologize for my short-sighted remark about putting Tybor on a farm."

I let the silence fall between us for a moment before I said, "Apology accepted."

"My father taught us that was the way. If I have any Omega siblings, I don't know about them. Any of them."

"That is a belief practiced by many families," I replied dryly. I took my hands off my stomach and leaned forward. "Every child deserves a father's love."

"Oh, well, I'm not sure my father would agree." He let out a pained laugh.

"I'm sorry about that."

"I can't complain. I was raised in utter luxury. Servants. All the best things. Never needed for anything. When I moved out on my own, I had to learn how to use a dishwasher and not let things sit in the fridge until they spoiled."

"Every kid has to learn those things, though."

"It was a bit late for me."

92

"Do you want to follow in your father's footsteps. Be like him?"

Mathias looked down. "I thought I did."

"I'm sure he's a very respected and important man. Someone you looked up to like a god."

"Even gods can have flaws," he replied.

"Yes. But the son doesn't necessarily inherit them by design. You say you're not a good guy? That's entirely by choice."

Chapter Eleven

Mathias

"Entirely by choice," Saber said.

Flawed not by design? Yet, I had been born into glamour and wealth. Privilege and expectation. One didn't undo that in a day. Kris had had change forced upon him overnight. And gentle Trigg? He'd been blindsided, but always the sweetheart of our trio, he quietly navigated all the bumps in the road.

Everything I can't have. Don't have. That's what Saber represented to me.

Now that I had opened my eyes, now that I couldn't get his bright hair and steady hazel gaze out of my mind, I realized I wanted him more than anything in my entire life.

I thought I had everything and I was still bitter. Unhappy. Looking to Father for guidance. Omegas, to my mind, were for breeding; it was what they were made for. I couldn't relate to that and had dismissed half the population as a result.

Full of hate and spite. That's what I'd become. I was filled with incredible animosity. Anger from places I couldn't define.

It was strange how light I'd felt today as I looked forward to the dinner at Saber's house. I'd shopped for the groceries and gifts with a kind of focus that brought with it continuous pumps of energy through my chest.

Now, as Saber talked to me, I wondered: Was this what normal people felt? People who weren't raised by trillionaire fathers who controlled their every move, who taught them about emotionless breeding, who defined heaven to be what was contained in the dark shadows of over-filled bank vaults?

"Choices. They seem vaster yet less complicated when you're young," I said.

"That's true." Saber smiled and that smile was like a light coming on inside my mind. "You don't think of the consequences as much when you're young."

I stared at him. He was a pregnant Omega, and I realized he found himself in a position where his choices had become perhaps more limited, but every move he made affected other lives, specifically, those of his kids and the ones on the way.

My choices seemed always to be about saving face with Father, and not caring what corners I cut to do it.

"Why do I care so much about what my father thinks?" I said it more to myself than to Saber.

"Seems to me maybe you have a lot to lose. A way of life? That's huge."

I nodded.

"But are you happy? Isn't that the biggest question anybody ever asks of their life?"

That question came with an easy answer. But when I didn't give it, Saber hopped up.

"Let's have that dessert," he said quickly.

I sat with my head forward on one hand, my elbow on the table, and this time I did not offer to help.

I heard dishes chiming with spoons. Saber came out with two plates containing apple pie with vanilla ice cream on top. He set one in front of me with a silver fork and one at his own place. Then he went back into the kitchen and called out, "Boys. Can you put your movie on pause, please, and come get your dessert?"

"Yay!" came two high-pitched voices from the living room.

The boys ran in and grabbed their dishes. "Ice cream for you guys," Saber said. "Today the pie is for the grown ups."

Without arguing, they each went to their places at the table and started eating, immediately getting ice cream all over their hands and faces, but smiling bright as if they'd just been gifted the sun.

Much as I'd seen them as a hindrance the first day we'd met at the bank, I'd taken a complete opposite view of them in the past two days. Saber kept them well in line, and obviously they were well-loved.

As we ate, Tybor started telling us about the cartoon movie they'd chosen to watch. Saber had no doubt seen this movie before, probably a hundred times, but his patience at letting Tybor speak, and asking him questions at pertinent points, was endearing. I hardly wanted to admit it, but I hadn't felt such contentment in a long, long time.

When the boys finished and went back to their movie, Saber cleared the dishes.

There was nothing left for me to do. I had no more reason to stay.

I stood at the kitchen island and watched Saber for a minute. "I should probably get going."

"What?" He rinsed his hands and dried them on a towel. "Oh."

"I've got a board meeting tomorrow, and--" I stopped. He didn't need to hear all the boring details.

"Let me walk you to the door." Was that disappointment I heard in his voice?

We walked down the short, wide hall and past the living room. In the foyer, Saber stepped up to open the door. As he did, he said, "It just seems so soon. That you're leaving, I mean."

His hand was on the doorknob. He hadn't turned it.

"The dinner was, uh." I searched for a word to describe it. "Extraordinary."

"Thank you."

I watched his face darken with a slight flush. We stood staring at each other, a tangible heat growing between us. He was beautiful in the shadows of the closed front door, the light from the TV in the living room just beyond flickering around him.

I should have been bold. Instead, Saber was the one to find his words first. "Is it just me, or is there—do you actually, maybe, kind of *want* to stay longer?"

"You have the boys, and, well." I stopped. What was I doing? "Maybe yes?"

"The boys' bedtime is seven-thirty. It's just after seven right now."

Could it be possible he wanted me the way I wanted him? And in what exact way was that?

For me, when I'd had sex with Omegas outside my Burn, it had been with strangers, furtive and fast, hard and emotionless. I didn't want them because I liked them. I wanted them because I was feeling crazy or drunk or pissed. Whatever. It wasn't something I gave much thought to.

I wanted Saber in every way opposite of that. I wanted him because he was smart, capable, and not overtly flirting. I wanted him because he was the most handsome Omega I'd ever seen, of course. I didn't ever hide the fact I was shallow in that way. But I had seen more in him, his heart when he was with his boys, his mind when he'd made no secret of the fact that he could handle himself quite well without a financial guardian.

Everything about Saber was opposite from what Father had taught me about proper family, and about how Omegas were.

If I'd been blind my whole life, Saber was the one to remove the blindfold.

"Do you really want to see where this will lead?" I asked. My voice sounded gravelly, almost emotionless. But I knew nothing of romance. Of softer words.

"I think I do," he answered. "Come on."

I left my leather case by the front door and followed him into the living room. The boys looked up as we entered.

"Are you staying for the movie?" Tybor asked me.

"I am," I replied, glancing at Saber to make sure. Saber nodded.

Both boys were sitting on the couch. Tybor scooted closer to his brother and said, "You can sit by me."

I obeyed the little Omega's command. Both boys had their toy kittens next to them on the couch. They couldn't have been cuter. At one time I would have laughed at myself for that thought. But tonight, no. The longing that swept over me for this little family was unlike anything I'd ever experienced.

I sat beside Tybor, who grinned up at me. Saber sat in a recliner to my left.

Whatever was playing on the TV was colorful and obnoxious but I didn't care.

"And what is the name of this glorious piece of film work we are watching?"

"Film what?" Saber chuckled. "The movie is called *Rascal Rabbit and the Two-Headed Peanut Butter Sandwich.*"

I couldn't help but glance at Saber with a questioning smirk.

He chuckled. "It's a classic," he said. Then rolled his eyes.

I said to Tybor, "I didn't know peanut butter sandwiches had heads. Let alone two."

Tybor and Luke giggled. "It's a cartoon," said Tybor.

"I see that."

"They save the world," said Luke softly.

"That's wonderful. It's good to save the world sometimes."

"All the time," Tybor insisted.

"All the time," I echoed in agreement. All of a sudden my heart clenched again at the memory that I had said the worst thing possible to Saber—that Tybor should be sent away to a chattel farm.

I was not the good guy. I never had been. Saber had forgiven me, but could I forgive myself?

Chapter Twelve

Saber

I couldn't help but watch the clock.

When the cartoon was over, I said to my twins, "Go get into your PJs and brush your teeth. I'll be in in a minute."

"Can we stay up a little bit, Daddy?" asked Luke.

"Not tonight.

It was funny how quickly they could move when they wanted to watch a movie, but how much they dragged their bodies when they were told to go and prepare for bed.

When Mathias and I were alone, I expected the awkwardness to resume between us. Instead, Mathias turned to me, his features softened more than I thought possible, and said, "You're really good with them."

"My boys are everything to me."

"I see that." He lifted his lips in a small but gorgeous smile. "Admirable."

"It's just called being a parent."

"But not all parents know how to be parents."

"True." I stood, stretching a little, hands self-consciously going to the small bump of my stomach. "I have to go see to them. I'll be back in a few minutes. Watch the TV or whatever you want."

I confess I rather hurried the boys through their bedtime routine. I didn't feel guilty, though. I'd been lonely for too long since way before Drayden passed. I wanted a pleasant evening with an Alpha I was attracted to. I deserved it.

But I still felt my pregnancy might get in the way. I was in shape, but my usual flat belly was gone. It still had firmness, it was just rounder now. Would he notice? Would he care?

Nerves, excitement, apprehension and wonder all vied for top space in my brain.

When the boys were down and their door closed, I walked back into the living room where Mathias sat idly channel surfing. He switched the TV off when I approached. The room dimmed.

I sat down next to him and said, "I'm glad you stayed."

"Are you?"

I frowned. "I asked you, didn't I?"

"I am probably not the man you are looking for for anything meaningful." His eyes lowered showing long lashes which made shadows on his proud cheekbones.

"When did I say I was? And besides, you wouldn't presume to tell me what I'm looking for, would you?"

"No. But I'm a little fucked up and--"

"Who isn't?" I interrupted. Drayden had been one fucked up Alpha. He couldn't be soft. He had to prove himself and work all the time. His Burns were like chores for him to get through, when I thought they should have brought us more intimacy, made us closer.

I was perhaps tired of meeting Alphas who hated themselves, but I wasn't done with that lesson in my life apparently, for here was one before me and my mouth went dry and my throat choked with want for him.

Maybe it was pheromones, or some combination of his generosity in doing things for me and the kids. Maybe it was my pregnancy hormones. I had no clue; I simply knew I wanted him. The urge came on stronger the more I allowed myself to feel it.

"Maybe I should just go," he said, his voice almost a whisper. He started to stand.

"Mathias, wait." My heart was hammering in my chest. I lifted my hand to his and grasped it. "Before you leave I want you to do one more thing for me."

His eyebrows quirked up.

I stood and turned to face him, still holding his hand. "You've already done so much for me. I have no right to ask for even more."

As I spoke I could see his face change. As if he wanted to do whatever I asked. As if he were compelled.

I knew Alphas. Somewhat. I knew their protective instincts, when awakened, could be stronger impulses than sex drives. If that urge was focused on one Omega for a time period, even a few days they would yearn to see to that Omega's needs.

Drayden had had it while we were courting, but once he knocked me up and had gotten his family and me as the live-in maid to take care of them, he focused on his career and our bond never fully formed.

"Ask," was all Mathias said, eyes locked on mine, not looking away.

"Kiss me. Just once. That's all." *That's all?* I couldn't believe I'd said that. I wanted so much more. But I had to see. Were we compatible? If the kiss tanked and was only lips on lips, just a gesture, I'd know. If it made my blood rush, I'd know something else.

"You are making sure," he said. It was not a question.

I shrugged. "I want you to."

He gave me a slow blink. Languid. Sexy as hell. Then he did something not even Drayden had ever done. He put one hand on my cheek and the other behind my neck, held my face in place, and leaned in.

The sensation of being held steady, of being controlled like that, made me dizzy before his lips brushed mine.

When the fullness of his mouth rested against mine, warm and tentative, a surge of heat shot through me. My whole body suffused with a kind of fever I'd longed to feel again, and hadn't in years.

My arms were limp at my sides, but now I brought them up. Before I touched his sides, before I turned this tentative gesture into a full embrace, I asked myself one single question.

What if this is only for tonight? Can you handle it?

My body said yes. My mind was a little slower to agree, but I made a pact with myself to enjoy this man, and if nothing came of it, it would be a sweet memory and nothing more.

We stood together for longer than I thought he would be willing to. With his strange hesitancy, and his closed up emotional demeanor, I thought he'd pull away pretty quickly.

His palms moved from my head down to my shoulders, the fingers gripping at the cloth of my shirt. They tightened and I could feel his nails scraping through the cloth. My skin shivered all the way down my arms which were wrapped around his waist and pressing.

He was solid and warm, but also like hugging stone, the muscles rigid and curved in all the right places. All Alpha. Damn if I couldn't help but be completely into him when just three days ago I had thought he was an ass.

I wasn't a small Omega, but I had to keep my head turned up to him to continue the kiss. His grip increased and just when I thought he would move his lips to encase mine, he pulled back, exhaling and turning his head. His eyes were closed, his mouth open just a quarter inch.

My cock had warmed and risen in my pants. I so wanted to adjust myself but I didn't dare move.

Mathias was an Alpha with problems. I didn't care. I wanted to know him better because over the last couple days I could see he had a big heart. Someone or something had crushed it along the way. His father probably.

Alphas with father problems were a dime a dozen. Yes, I thought to myself. If this went further, or was only for tonight, I could handle it.

Chapter Thirteen

Mathias

I'd never gotten so hard so fast for an Omega outside the burn than I was now with Saber. Nameless, faceless encounters in dark rooms at brothels or adult parties didn't faze me. But this—this had *stuff* opening up inside me I'd never felt before.

I wanted it. Because of that, I had something here to lose. This feeling. This warmth. This household with a family that was so different from what I had been used to my whole life.

If I made a wrong move, would I ever have this sensation again?

I'd never frozen up like this about sex before. My personal issue with knotting was my own close-held secret and my partners never needed to know, so that wasn't it.

Saber felt so right, my hands on his shoulders, his around my waist. He smelled amazing, like fresh soap and distant rain, and again that sweet lilac scent. I wanted to kiss him again. I wanted to take him, wholly, make him feel what I felt. I'd never had this urge before, not once, to make an Omega feel something—or anything—beyond my dick in their ass.

But with Saber, I wanted to worship him. That sort of desire didn't happen to me.

Was this what my brother Kris felt with his bondmate Thorne? Was it something one experienced all the time? Because Father never had a mate, I figured it was something rare, or a lot of talk blowing mate-bonding out of proportion.

Now Saber stood before me, patient, waiting. I saw only dark wave after dark wave of empty yearning behind my closed eyelids.

I wanted him. This wasn't just any Omega, but a pregnant Omega with two kids. Nothing I'd ever imagined wanting.

I opened my eyes, keeping them downcast, then moving them up from his chest to his face.

His arms around my waist. Firm. Hard. His upturned chin. His stormy hazel eyes darkened by the wide pupils. His hair wafting gently across his forehead in shining, blond wisps.

Mine. I tugged on his shoulders. He came toward me easily, his head turning slightly, and brushed his cheek against my chin. A soft sigh escaped him.

Flames licked their way through my body. I dared to press my face to his, moving until our noses touched and my mouth could claim him for real this time. More demanding. More open.

He accepted without hesitation, his lips forming to mine. That was it. My mind spun away until I lost all sense of time, place, self.

There were moments I found my hands back in his hair. Moments I heard him moan deep within his throat. That moment when his thigh slid against mine and his hip pushed against my erection.

Two kisses only and the room had to be in ashes around us. It was that warm.

Finally, we pulled back for air. Saber looked up at me, his lips pressed hard as he sucked on them, his eyes sparkling. He was the most gorgeous being I'd ever known.

"Would you like to see my bedroom again? Unofficially this time."

I could only nod.

He let out a small laugh of pure joy, took my hand and led me down the hall past the baby room, past his office and the twins' room, and into his bedroom with the purple spread and dark curtains.

All the way there it seemed as if I walked on air.

We stood in front of his big bed facing each other. Saber reached up and put his hands on the lapels of my jacket, pushing the material up and off my shoulders. When I let my blazer drop from my hands he caught it, ran his palm and over it gently, and placed it over the back of a nearby chair.

He then began to undo the buttons on my shirt. He was moving slowly, thoughtfully, which simply would not do.

I took over, unbuttoning the rest of my shirt until it fell open revealing my bare skin to the air. Then I reached for the hem of his shirt and pulled it up.

Saber's hands were already on my belt.

We rushed, then, tugging and pulling, stepping out of shoes, socks and pants.

He went to the side of the bed and tugged at the plush spread. I followed him, taking him into my arms, kissing him again as we both fell on our sides.

He was light tan all over, lovely, so lovely, and now I reveled in the fact that I was allowed to run my hands all over his sides and back.

When I came to the front, he pulled back from the kiss.

"I'm a little self-conscious," he said, looking down.

"Why?"

He just smiled.

Then I remembered. He was five months pregnant. It was hard to remember that since the clothing he wore fit him well and showed little of his bump. He was slim and muscular.

I ran my hand down his chest to his stomach. The skin gleamed softly and my fingertips tingled. I could see it now. The gentle rise of his abdomen, the slight stretch of his bellybutton. But the skin was like satin, so smooth, and muscular. His stomach was firm, not soft, and within grew life, something of him, from him, real and alive.

I never thought such a sight would fascinate me. But I was completely enamored. I didn't get enamored, so what was wrong with me? Deep within me welled a need and a hunger to clutch, hold, protect, save. How could this be happening? The sons he carried weren't even mine.

This was a hook up. Nothing more. Wasn't it?

But it was more than that. Something deeper that was grinding into my soul like a corkscrew, implanting itself in a way that was too tangled and invasive to ignore.

Where was this coming from? I would dismiss it all if I were a few days off from my next Burn. But I'd just had a Burn and wasn't due for another two months.

I couldn't help myself. I reached out and ran my hands over his belly, circling.

He fell onto his back and moaned.

I shoved my fingers underneath the waistband of his briefs and slid them over his hips and off.

So beautiful, he was, lying naked before me, his body glowing in the low lights, mouth open, eyes glimmering. His cock was pink and pretty, darker at the tip, and fully hard. It was picture perfect, like a dream. I wanted to touch. To hold. To stroke. To taste. I couldn't breathe. All I could think, again, was, *Mine.*

Chapter Fourteen

Saber

Mathias put a warm hand on my rounded belly and kept it there for a long time. I almost pushed him away. I couldn't help the self-conscious feeling that came over me, as if my pregnant stomach might change his mind about wanting me. He was an Alpha. Privileged. Spoiled. He could have anyone. At five months along, I carried toward the back and didn't show all that much, but still I was aware my belly was not flat.

I was used to being in good shape. I loved my boys and being a dad, but I was not necessarily fond of being pregnant, or flaunting it.

"Ignore that," I whispered.

"Shh." It came out a brief hiss. "Let me."

Whatever that meant.

I closed my eyes at the gentleness, the care, something so unexpected I felt heat begin to pool in the backs of my eyes. Arcing electrical currents crisscrossed in my belly and at the base of my spine. My cock throbbed, already fully erect. Something about the tips of his fingers there. Something about the curve of his large palm. Something about the way it felt as if he wanted to protect me and my kids, all of us, Tybor and Luke, and the little ones still inside me beating their hearts in tune with my own.

My cock pulsed with blood.

"Ah," he said, and moved his hand downward.

He ran his palm over the underside, up and down. Everything in me wanted him. My balls ached. My ass slickened. I started to turn.

"No," he said softly, bending his head to kiss the skin just below my pecs. "Lie back."

He didn't want to fuck me? "It won't hurt the babes," I said softly.

He did not reply.

He caressed me lightly. He leaned over me and stared down into my eyes, his own so black in the shadowy room, but glistening. His braid lightly slapped against my side and I wanted to undo it, wanted so badly to feel his hair woven through my fingers like rippling black water.

As he ran his hands up and down my swollen cock and kissed my chest, I grabbed his braid, pulling a little.

He raised his head, hand still on my cock, and watched me undo the band at the end and toss it. Then my hands unraveled the weave. It slid apart easily and my fingers went into his hair, combing.

The softness of it was like a child's hair, fine and light, although much thicker.

As I played in his hair, he lowered his head and before I knew what he was going to do, he took my cock in his mouth, letting its length slide into him as he softly sucked it in.

"Ahhh!" My hips arched up.

Most Alphas wanted only to fuck. Including Drayden. Which was fine. It was what Omegas were made for. I'd sucked Drayden only a few times in our entire marriage, and that was only if he wanted me to ready him quickly. Drayden had never offered to return the favor.

I didn't expect differently from Mathias despite his unnerving gentleness with me when he kissed me and didn't rush me, taking his seduction slowly. But I didn't expect this! Never before had I had oral sex performed upon me. It was amazing.

My hands tightened in Mathias's long hair, pulling. He sucked down further until his mouth was around my root.

I didn't realize I'd pulled so hard on his locks until he grunted.

"Sorry!" I nearly sat up.

His hand shot out and pushed me on the chest to settle back. He grunted, moving his mouth up and gods I was lost. Completely taken over by pleasure, my head spun, my eyes closed and the blackness of the insides of my eyelids was speckled with bright white lights.

"Oh gods," I breathed. "Oh!"

The hand on my chest moved lower to caress my round belly again as he moved his head up and down. It was incredible.

My grip on his long hair did not let up, and he did not protest as I put my hands against his head, holding him as he moved to take me deep again.

He pulled up after a good long suck and his tongue circled the head of my cock, all around, back and forth, dipping into the cleft at the tip.

My balls drew up as his mouth engulfed me again in hard, indrawn pressure.

Up he came again, giving luscious attention to the head. I couldn't take it.

"I'm—I'm going to—I can't hold back!" I yelled, gripping tighter to his head.

I figured he'd pull off then, let me spurt into the air.

Instead, he sucked my length down fast and I saw stars.

My cock throbbed hard and shot. And shot again. Right down his throat.

His hand went to the base of my cock and his fingers surrounded it, milking as he came up and suckled the head.

The pulses returned and as he took his head away I felt my semen still dribbling from the tip. It had been months since I'd last had a lover. Drayden had died just before his next Burn. I'd been almost three months pregnant when he died. It hadn't been long enough for me to give much thought to having another Alpha lover, at least not at this time in my life.

"Give it all to me," Mathias said huskily, putting his mouth over the tip again and sucking lightly, teasing.

"Shit!"

Another throb came when he milked, another pulse burst from the tip.

I had been one hard up little Omega.

He pulled back a bit. "That's it," he said. "All of it." And licked and licked until I couldn't stand it anymore and begged him to stop.

"Do you really want me to stop?" he asked, hand coming to my belly again, and rubbing.

He moved up in the bed, his mouth kissing along my ribs and then latching onto one of my hard nipples. His tongue and lips caressed it, leaving me still writhing as he finally took me into his arms and found my mouth with his own.

Tongues collided.

I couldn't breathe. I didn't care.

I had a craving to touch myself again. Apparently I hadn't had enough.

My ass leaked with 'honey' as most Alphas had called it.

As he kissed, I reached between us, feeling his big, firm erection.

I leaned back. "Fuck me," I said.

"Insatiable *and* demanding."

"Fuck yes," I agreed. "But it is your turn, too." I sat up.

"Are you sure in your condition?"

"It told you. It's okay. Really. Have you never been with a pregnant Omega?"

He shook his head.

"It's actually good for us hormonally to have this, uh, this sort of affection. And stretching is good. All the way up to the birth." My face heated at the words.

I could see his cock bobbing in the shadowy dimness. Big and fully hard. Thick like I liked them when I was young on the chattel farm and serviced Alpha Burns.

At the root of his cock, Mathias wore a silver ring. I had heard of cock-rings, of course, but never seen one in person and on an actual man standing before me. The idea that he wore it, and had had it on all this time, turned me on even more than I already was.

Mathias rolled between my legs, pushing my thighs apart and up, tugging a pillow into place beneath my hips.

My hole leaked. I wanted an ass orgasm this time, already anticipating the wave it could produce like a tsunami. To help him, I put my hands around my own thighs and pulled them close to my chest.

I was open and ready, my ass ready for him. Tingling, wet.

Mathias put his hand there to feel and assess. "You're a wet little sweetheart, aren't you?"

I couldn't believe how much his endearment turned me on. He couldn't have played more into my fantasies if he tried. "Put it in me," I commanded, arching up.

Without hesitation, he positioned himself. The head of his large cock pressed my entrance. So big. So hard. What my body craved.

He grabbed my shoulder with one hand, and with his other on his cock, aimed into me and pushed.

I felt the entry with every inch, a smooth but quite large intrusion. My hole stretched to take him, soaked and ready, but it was still a lot. Mathias was big. Heavily ripped. His body pressed mine with such a fierce, earnest need it made my flesh grow hot and cold all over. Gorgeous. Fervent. Feverish even without the Burn. He was everything I dreamed of, and that I hadn't dared to ever dream of having.

My sensitive insides became immediately stimulated, and my muscles eased up to let him all the way in. When he was seated, my ass pulsed all around him.

"Fuck," he whispered. "What are you doing?"

"It feels so good. My body can't help it."

"Squeezing me like that?" He pressed himself forward until his face was at my neck, his breath warm on my jaw and ear. "I've never felt so... so welcome."

"What? But don't all Omegas--"

He cut me off. "I guess not," he hissed, sucking at my skin and no doubt leaving a pleasure bruise right below my ear.

What kinds of experiences had this man been having with Omegas his whole life? I thought all Omega's ass muscles milked their partners. I quickly lost that thought as his cock grew bigger inside me.

I couldn't help my response to him. His cock stimulated every Omega nerve along my passage. My hole gripped him as if my body never wanted to let him go.

For a long time he didn't move. Maybe he couldn't. Maybe he didn't want to.

Finally, he broke the silence.

"Take a breath," he whispered.

As I drew air into my lungs, he pulled out very slowly.

I cried out in pleasure as his cock brushed my prostate as well as the secretion glands that wept natural lubricant when invigorated by an Alpha's erect, thrusting penis.

"Oh," he said. Just that one word.

"Oh gods yes, fuck me!" I yelled in a strangled voice.

His hips moved.

I let go of the grip on my thighs and both my hands reached for his hips, my fingertips digging into his buttocks, pulling him to me.

He eased in, then out again, my hands pulling and pushing to the rhythm we set, and he fucked me so thoroughly and beautifully I saw dark colors begin to emerge in the air, my vision all wonky, drugged from pleasure.

I clutched at his ass which was firm and muscled, ran my fingers up and down to his thighs to marvel at the hard muscles there as well, the incredible strength.

"Ah, you are beautiful," I heard him whisper. "So wet. So warm. So tight when you do that thing--"

Whatever I was doing—milking him with my ass?—I didn't know I was doing it. All I understood was that the pleasure caused me to undulate against him, making me crave more and more.

With every thrust, his cock grazed all my pleasure zones. Impossibly, even my spent cock was hard again, slapping my belly as he moved within me.

Mathias lifted his head and kissed me. "I can't hold back. I'm going to come." His voice came breathless in the shadows when he broke away.

"Don't hold back."

"It'll be hard and fast," he said breathlessly.

"Do it!" I gripped his hips harder as he pushed in and out of me fast, faster, until I thought I'd pass out from the sheer joy of it.

His hips shuddered up and down and his thrusts became deep and lightning quick, like a piston.

Mathias gave a broken cry and I felt him freeze inside me, his big cock growing and growing until it pulsed and my insides felt the flood of his boiling ecstasy.

My channel clenched and I came, too, internally this time, the shock of it traveling up my spine until I went rigid with the orgasm, locked in place.

It was so good. The best sex ever. I guess I'd had a lot of only passable sex in my youth.

I half expected him to knot, but after a minute he pulled out, cock wet and gleaming in the low lighting, the silver ring glimmering, hand on my ass caressing upward to my balls.

He saw my hard cock and bent between my legs.

This time when he took it into his mouth I was sure nothing would happen. I was replete with exhaustion, limp everywhere but my dick which, in my past experiences, would soften very quickly as I relaxed in afterglow. But when his mouth touched me, tongue against the head, lips surrounding me, saliva slicking me,

113

the pleasure slammed up through me again. His hand tugged lightly on my balls.

I screamed in a low, loud voice as he sucked sweetly and lightly, as if he knew I was over stimulated and trying to be gentle, until my whole cock filled his mouth. I shot hard as he drank from me. Thirsty bastard.

I'd never come so many times in a row like that in a single session with an Alpha. This time: twice externally, once internally. Usually if I came more than once with an Alpha it was only after I'd rested for a while.

I looked up as his mouth popped off the head of my cock, licking the last of my drip, sucking it clean and dry. My skin glistened with sweat. His body rippled in the light, his cock hard again.

I trembled and dozed for a few minutes and heard him get up, then later felt a towel rubbing me down.

Finally, when I could move, I opened my eyes and just stared at him. What had we done? It didn't seem like simple sex. Like getting off. It was more like making love.

He was on his knees looking down at me and a new look came over his face, one I hadn't seen before. Maybe it was the dim lighting. Maybe it was my blurred vision. But something had taken away all the angles and sharpness of his cheeks, jaw, nose and mouth and replaced it with soft wonder. His lips were half open, still damp.

His cock stuck up hard and dry,—he'd wiped it clean of my juices with the towel—and jutted from its thatch of curly black hair and encircled by the ring of silver.

Finding energy I did not know I had, I brought myself up and pushed him onto his back, my hands on his thighs and pulling them apart. I put his cock in my mouth and sucked down, cupping his balls and gently rippling my fingers beneath them.

He fell onto the pillows with a grunt, thrusting up into my mouth.

Time lost all meaning, but it didn't feel like I sucked him for long, my mouth stretched over his girth, my

114

throat aching to take the length, before he came in great pulsings into my mouth.

I swallowed the rich, tartness of him as fast as I could. When I pulled off, licking the dark, round head, he was still so hard. But no knot. Was the ring maybe getting in the way?

Alphas didn't knot every time they came, so that was fine. But I did love that fact about them, that ability to gather all sensation and ecstasy into the base of their cock and swell with it, holding onto the orgasm, continuing to pulse as the knot worked up the shaft and gave its last, strong burst at the head of the cock.

I stroked him gently, marveling at the girth and weight of him, the smooth, veined texture, the plush softness of the large, rounded head. Just to be sure he wouldn't start to knot late, I ran my hand down again, gripping him at the root and stroking my fingers against the ring.

As I did that, he grunted, then whispered, "You're wonderful."

I grinned up at him, moving over his body, dragging my exhausted cock along his thigh.

He grabbed me and brought me into a cradle hold, one arm around my back, the other pulling my legs up and over his thighs. He held me tight. My cheek rested against his big chest. He smelled like sex and Alpha and fiery wind. I breathed deep.

This was what I'd always wanted but wasn't sure existed. This. The merging of two bodies, the heat, the pleasure, the extreme contentment. The lovemaking. Was that what we'd just done?

His hand coming up from underneath me and onto my shoulder pulled me closer to him.

I clutched him with my free arm over his chest and tucked the other beneath his trim waist.

His hand on my thigh gripped, his fingers long enough to press my ass cheek. He caressed me there. It felt possessive, protective. And so very very right.

This was so intimate for someone I'd just met. Almost too intimate. Yet I wanted it. Wanted him and only him.

His nose was in my hair. I felt his breath scour my scalp, and his body beneath my weight relaxed as I fell into a deep stupor and then blank sleep.

Chapter Fifteen

Mathias

When he ran his hands down the shaft of my cock to the base, I knew Saber was feeling for my knot that never came and never had come in my whole life.

I grabbed him into my arms, a gesture I hadn't done before with any Omega, and held him to me. I gave myself various excuses as to why I did this: I wanted to continue to feel his exquisite body. I was a little bit chilly. I wanted another round of sex.

In truth, I couldn't part from him just yet. And it wasn't sexual. I wanted to hold him to me, yes, and I thought I might never tire of having sex with this man, but beyond that some deeper instinct had me wanting to wrap myself around him and never let go. To guard, protect, keep. To have as my own.

Saber clutched willingly to me, fitting into my arms as if made for me. His thigh slid over mine until both his legs were on me as if he sat in my lap, though we were both lying down. I had both my arms wrapped about his waist, my palms flat against his back.

He tucked his head in the crook of my neck, his blond hair tickling my nose.

This never happened to me. This couldn't happen. I wasn't looking for a relationship. Or feelings. Yet everything in me compelled me toward this Omega, this man, this widower who was simply trying to get by.

I saw myself as if from a distance. My lips caressed his hair. My breath fluttered the shining strands. I inhaled his sweet, blooming scent only to want it deeper inside me, a part of me.

My arms tightened around him.

Saber gave a little moan, half his face pressed to my chest.

I drifted, thinking about how heady he'd tasted, my lips around his perfect, gorgeous cock sucking. I wanted to do that again. And again.

My own cock was still half hard, nestled between us, content but wanting more. I dozed peacefully, feeling Saber's breath shush against my pecs in a rhythm that told me he was napping.

When I woke, darkness filled the room, and Saber had moved so that he was on his side, his forehead pressed to my shoulder, fast asleep. He must have gotten up at some point and turned off the lights and pulled the covers up.

Why hadn't he wakened me?

My body went rigid. What time was it? I wasn't sure I was invited to actually stay the whole night. Not knowing what to do, I tried to remember where I'd put my phone so I could check the time. As I moved to glance at the nightstand, I saw a digital clock glowing red to the side. It read 12:15.

Not too late.

I started to sit up.

Saber shifted beside me. "Hey." His voice came on soft currents of sleep. "You okay?"

"Yes."

"Do you need anything?"

You. More of you. "No. But I was—I was thinking."

Saber lifted his head. "Uh oh."

"No, don't." I stroked my fingers through his hair. "Just I was thinking I should go if you don't want the boys to see me when they wake in the morning."

"They're very young, but they know the word sleepover as it relates to kids. They'll think their daddy simply had a sleepover of his own."

But it was more than that. More than their daddy having a sleepover with a friend. At least it was to me. I

118

hoped Saber might think it, too. I wanted to voice his thoughts, but couldn't find the words.

I needed to wake up more, shake the mist from my brain. I wasn't thinking clearly.

"Mathias," Saber said softly. His breath brushed over my face. "You can stay for breakfast if you want."

"I—I shouldn't."

Why did I say that? I wanted to stay. I wanted to hold Saber more, feel him all up against me, his dizzying presence, his heat, his amazing response to me. I wanted to make sure everything was all right with him and his children, that he needed for nothing. I had the strangest instinct to puff out my chest and watch over him, rub against him, his bed, the walls of his house, marking my territory.

For me, this sort of behavior was completely out of the ordinary. It felt rude, unseemly.

"I don't want to overstay my welcome," I said, and realized my voice sounded low and inflectionless. I heard Father in that voice. People had called me cold for less.

Saber sat up, the covers falling away to reveal his silhouette, the shadows bathing him. I could see the fall of hair in his sleepy eyes, a lighter gilt upon the darkness.

My whole body seized up in warm currents of desire. My cock throbbed between my thighs. I reached out and brushed that soft hair from his face.

At the gesture, he leaned into to me and before I knew what I was doing I sought his mouth with my own, kissing, teasing with my tongue.

He fell against me and I was helpless. My arms went around him. I couldn't think. He climbed over my lap and straddled me. His lovely cock pressed hard to my belly, fully erect. His balls rubbed my pubic bone.

I placed one hand underneath him on the roundness of one buttock, and clutched. He rose up and teased my cock with his moves, rubbing his crack up and down the length. My erection stood straight up against his backside, twitching for him.

We kissed deeper, tongue dueling, his hands on my shoulders, his fingernails digging into my skin.

When he pulled back for breath, he said, "I'm slick. Put it in."

I could not resist as he drew up on his knees, bending to open himself, one hand going back to his ass and grabbing one cheek while I pulled on the other to spread him. I fingered him to be sure, and he was slippery and hot, two fingers going easily into him. I pulled them out and filled the gap with the head of my cock, steering it, the tip touching him gently. Oh so wet. So finely slick.

I felt his palm on the underside of my cock, pressing, holding it straight up as he lifted himself and impaled himself on it, his body sinking down on it in such heat I threw my head back, gritted my teeth and moaned.

Hands back on my shoulders now, he balanced himself and began to move his hips, his hole taking me in and immediately moving up to milk me, then going back down again. He fucked himself on me slow at first, his breaths coming in gasps and short bursts.

We kissed as he took me into himself over and over, letting me lie there and not do any of the work, his own wet cock slapping at my belly.

My Omega moved up and down, up and down. My knees bent in pleasure, my legs spreading between his thighs. I was on my back now, and Saber bounced on me, groaning, one hand coming up and brushing at my hair, touching my cheek.

"You're so hard," he whispered. "It's fantastic."

"You feel so good. So hot, so tight." I never talked like this during sex.

His internal muscles massaged my cock endlessly, never letting up. I wanted to move my hips and rut up against him, but I didn't want this moment to end with him moving upon me, taking control, my Omega pleasuring himself as I lost my mind.

My Omega.

120

When had I started calling him that?

Saber moved upon me, his hips lifting up and down, his upper body bending toward me, lips on mine slipping, sliding low to my jaw, my neck.

My hands gripped the sides of his thighs and moved along his ass, tugging his cheeks apart as if to get inside him deeper. The dark room spun around me. I moaned until I lost my breath. I never wanted this to end.

But the peak was coming. I felt it from my toes to the top of my head, along my spine, in the tremble of my abdomen and the tightening of my balls.

Saber's juices ran so swiftly now my entire groin was wet. He slipped and slid on my cock, his fucking becoming faster, more powerful.

He was a strong little guy, and I loved that he sought his pleasure on me, with me.

I couldn't hold back any longer. His moans and mine filled the air.

For a stark moment, I worried we'd wake the boys. But Saber seemed unconcerned about that. Plus, he'd locked the door. If the little ones woke, they'd knock if they needed their daddy.

Banishing the thought, I focused on Saber now, how he nuzzled my jaw, how he groaned from deep inside, how his ass rode my cock like he couldn't get enough. My fingers dug into the flesh of his buttocks, spreading him wider, and he hissed. "Yes, touch me. Touch me!"

I spread my hands around his hole, fingers sliding alongside it and my own cock as it went in and out of him. I pulled one hand forward and squeezed it between us to grasp his cock.

He gave a higher pitched keen when I milked him with my fist. He sat up and I milked him root to tip, rubbing my thumb along his head, feeling the drip there and sliding the tip of my thumb against the tiny hole.

He bounced hard, taking me all the way in. His muscles clenched me tight and his sweet cock burst in my hand as he came both externally and internally at the same time.

"Ah, gods," he cried out. "I'm coming. It's so good. Both ways. Coming!"

The idea that he was experiencing double pleasure, and with his Omega glands gripping me in undulating waves, sent me over the edge.

I came hard, filling him up with my own emissions, hot and jetting hard inside him.

Amazed and dazed, I lay back, my cock still twitching inside him as he gently and slowly pulled off me and fell to his side.

He reached between my legs and milked me dry, saying softly, "Are you done?"

"I don't know if I'll be done with you for a while, yet," I replied.

"No, I mean--" He stopped.

It occurred to me he was asking if I was going to knot.

My cheeks heated at the thought he might find out I had never done that. Me. A thirty year old Alpha. Never knotting. It was an embarrassment Omegas at the chattel farms where I cooled my Burns never seemed to notice. Probably because I took charge and never let up until I was done with them. If I kept fucking them, they didn't have time to notice knots, or the lack thereof.

To distract him, I said, "That was wonderful. I'm great. It's great."

He sighed, smiling through the darkness. I could see a gleam of teeth, a flash of his eyes before he nuzzled into my shoulder again and promptly fell to sleep.

For a long while I lay holding him against me, thinking I should leave. He'd invited me to breakfast but it didn't feel right. The boys would see I'd stayed over. They'd have questions and even though Saber said they would understand, I didn't like the idea of it. I didn't like the feeling. It was all too much, too fast. Too close.

Yet the protective urge came over me again, even stronger than before. I moved my face into Saber's fine hair and breathed in. Lilacs. It must be his shampoo. It mixed with the lingering scents of hot sex. And oh had it been hot.

But I needed to go.

The effort to drag myself away from Saber's body and his bed was staggering. I had to muscle my way through it both physically and mentally.

My legs felt like they weighed a ton as I pulled on my underwear and trousers. My arms became heavy in my shirtsleeves, tugging at my neck.

I felt the bed move as I bent to put on my shoes, but when I turned to look, Saber was still fast asleep, sprawled across two pillows, his shining hair gleaming in the dim light.

Finally dressed, I covered him with a blanket, then stalked like a guilty dog from his room.

The door lock sounded loud as it clicked. In the hall, my shoes made my footsteps too loud. But nothing moved. As I passed by the twins' room I heard nothing.

Once I got to the front door, I made sure the lock was secure as I left, wanting to know this little family was safe. Safe from the world of Alphas.

Safe from me.

Chapter Sixteen

Saber

A jolt of emptiness, like panic, shot through my solar plexus as I woke alone, my hands feeling the flatness of the mattress beside me where no Alpha lover lay, where there was only air.

Mathias was gone.

I don't know why I didn't waken to hear him leave. Sure, I'd come multiple times, harder than ever before, and was exhausted, but I chastised myself for not sensing, not knowing he would run. Not holding tighter to him.

I'd promised myself if this was just a hook-up I'd be okay. I had to be okay for my boys. All four of them.

I put my hand on my belly to feel the bump of the two still growing inside me. I rubbed to soothe both myself and them. Sometimes, lately, they'd become restless and it felt almost like indigestion, the fluttering, the feel of them curled within.

I wished I could bring them into the world with an Alpha father. But even if Drayden had lived, he was never home, always traveling, always flying.

Mathias was a fantasy. I knew it. But wow, how incredible the sex had been. How close and intimate. Already my body missed him. Just the thought of him had my heart beating faster, my skin fevering.

As I lay there staring at the ceiling, my knees spread at the memory of him between them, of him inside me so big and strong. My hole grew damp.

I glanced at the clock. Six-twenty. Much as I wanted to lie about and doze, I needed to get up, shower and start breakfast for the boys.

With a groan, and a slight twinge in my back that made me smile yet again at the memory of such fantastic sex, I got up and went to turn on the shower.

*

At breakfast, the boys ate heartily and didn't ask me any questions. Perhaps Mathias had been right to worry about what they would think if they knew he'd spent the night. Yet it felt wrong not to have him here, all dark and sinister, perhaps raising his eyebrows at my bacon and eggs, asking me for more.

My chest lurched, looking toward the empty chair he'd sat in just last night at dinner. Several times, as the kids ate, I looked at my phone, thinking of texting him. But I chickened out.

Back and forth my mind went on this single, simple act. Why should I wait for him to text? But if I initiated a text, would he be bothered by it? Would I be moving too fast?

Last night I felt the connection between us. More than just a casual encounter. Perhaps the attraction between us had been rather quick, but I would never have let it go any further if it had only been that. I wasn't looking for hook-ups in my life. And yet, I'd promised myself last night I'd be okay with it if that was Mathias's intent.

I stood at the kitchen counter, the sunlight streaming in through the plate glass windows from the backyard, and rocked back and forth.

"Daddy, I'm done," said Tybor from the table.

"Me, too," said Luke.

"Can we go out back to play?" Tybor asked.

"Go on, then." I opened the door for them and they ran out to their swing set, Luke stopping first to pick up a bright green plastic ball and toss it.

I cleared the table, then leaned against the counter facing out back and watched my boys run and play, chasing the ball, rolling in the grass, banging on the swings. I left the door open and their laughter floated in on the warm breeze.

I held my phone in my hand, glancing at it sporadically. Finally, I put it in my pocket and did a few household chores.

The kids came in every half hour asking for snacks or drinks. They were so energetic and demanding. I could barely focus on them, they moved so quickly, and I realized I was tired from last night, and for the first time feeling the lethargy of being pregnant as well.

Hearing nothing from Mathias also put me in a mentally apprehensive and worried state.

Stupid, I knew. Mathias had his own life. I had a family. We couldn't have been more opposite.

I prepared lunch and put it in the fridge to keep until lunchtime.

Listening to my children play, I went to the couch in the far alcove of the dining room and sat down, turning and putting my feet up.

Next thing I knew, I was jerking awake when I heard Tybor crying.

I sat up, dizzy for a moment. "Ty baby?"

My kids were standing in front of me. Tybor had tears on his cheeks and Luke stood next to him with his head down.

"Luke hit me." He held out his arm pointing to his wrist. "Right here."

"Did not!" Luke protested, his eyes filling with tears.

"Come here, you two."

They stepped forward.

I gently took Tybor's arm in my hand and kissed his wrist. "There. Boo-boo healed."

He sniffled.

I looked at Luke. "Now, what happened? Did you hit Tybor?"

"It was a assident."

"An accident?" I said slowly.

He nodded vigorously.

"Ty? Was it?"

"I guess he didn't mean to. We were playing ball and he tried to get it from me."

"So it was a game," I said. I brought them both into a hug. "Only a game. And everything is okay."

"Daddy. We're hungry. Is it lunch yet?" they asked in unison.

I grabbed my phone from my pocket and saw I'd slept about half an hour. I never did that! I sighed.

"Sure, boys. I have lunch all ready."

I sighed. I loved them deeply, but sometimes I got tired of the routines. Of talking to five year olds all day long. I went online sometimes for adult conversation but it wasn't enough.

Mathias had been perhaps more important company than I realized. I looked for any message from him but found none. If I didn't hear from him by the end of the day, I vowed I'd message him myself.

The kids filled the room with their energy, but somehow I felt empty, listless, aimless. I sent a mental message toward my phone. *Please call.*

It remained silent.

The kids bounced to their seats at the table. I got out their sandwiches and fruit and drinks and set it all up for them. I made myself some food as well, but I wasn't hungry.

I managed to eat half of my lunch while still staring at my silent phone.

"Daddy," Tybor said, his mouth full.

"Swallow before speaking," I gently reprimanded.

He made a big gulping sound, then said, "Is that big man who is helping us coming back?"

"The man from the bank?"

He nodded.

"I don't know, sweetie."

It was all I could say. Because I didn't know and with every hour that passed I grew less and less sure.

Chapter Seventeen

Mathias

I kept glancing at my phone seeing texts from everyone in my life but one. Saber. Not that I expected a text.

My office was quiet. Most of my work, when I did work, was on the computer. I didn't have to deal with people except during board meetings, which I showed up to as a representative for Father.

Trigg kept texting me.

I want to talk to you. Can we meet for lunch?

I put off answering him until I got three more. Who I really wanted to meet for lunch was Saber. But he had the kids and I had left without waking him and it seemed so abrupt. If I asked to see him again so soon, would he find me intrusive?

Father texted me about a few business items, which I took care of in minutes. He never mentioned the dinner he'd excused me from. He did not say a word about my outburst about Kris, nor did he threaten to oust me from job, money or his life.

It was as if that dinner had never happened. That was how Father handled things that made him uncomfortable. In the past, that was how I handled things as well. Anything I didn't like in my life I got rid of without further thought. I had what I wanted. I lived how I wanted. I indulged in nice fashion, food, vacations and that was my life. A little wild, a lot shallow and walking about like I was god of the bank, impressing people with my Vandergale name.

I had no complaints. Most people would kill for a life like mine. I never questioned any of it. And I'd justified my past bad behavior with Kris as proper for an Alpha because Father approved.

But one meeting with one little Omega who'd lost his mate and I was now questioning everything. I was very uncomfortable. Uncomfortable got swept under the rug. Before this, uncomfortable got put out of the mind.

Easier said than done.

How could I forget the glimmer of his blue eyes, the softness of his pale hair, the way he had arched when I sucked him, and the sweet, sweet taste? How could I not replay in my mind over and over the way he opened for me, the way his internal muscles milked my cock like no other Omega I'd ever been with? Or the way his arms held me afterward, and how he kissed so soft and deep, as if to burrow into me, the freshness of his warm mouth, his tongue curling against mine, his breath coming into me as if it were my own?

My body tingled and swelled and heated at every instant I thought of him.

I was glad of the privacy of my luxurious office, because I was hard more than I wasn't just sitting there at my computer. My face felt constantly warm.

I glanced again and again at my phone as it buzzed me messages all morning. Nothing important. Nothing from Saber.

I finally replied to Trigg.

You're a hard-ass that never lets up. I'll meet you at noon.

Then I texted him our favorite restaurant with extremely high-priced meals. His reply came in seconds.

See you there.

*

129

Trigg wore jeans and a nice jacket, no tie. But as he walked up the steps to the entrance, he pulled a tie out of his pocket. This establishment required them.

He wrapped his about his neck and expertly tied it in seconds. Father had taught us about ties when we were all very young. Had us practice the knots over and over until we were experts.

Trigg worked in design and architecture for one of Father's firms, and taught art several times a week at night school. He greeted me with a pleasant smile, his short, dark hair gelled so it stayed combed forward on the sides which were longer than the top.

Of all of us, he looked the most like Father, and the least. He had Father's chin and nose and eyes, but he was soft at the edges, relaxed and smooth in every way that Father was hard and controlled and tense.

"Math, finally! Have you been avoiding me or what?"

"Or what," I answered.

He came forward and hugged me. I let him because he always respected my solid stance of some discomfort and made his hugs brief and light.

"Let's go inside and you can tell me all about it."

"Hmmph." I followed him into the dim foyer.

At our usual table, the wine poured, Trigg sat back and stared at me for a long time.

"Stop that," I said. "Ass."

"Idiot," he replied softly. "Something's different about you and I'm trying to figure it out."

I remained silent.

"Is it because of the other night at Father's?"

"No." I scoffed. "That incident is forgotten."

"But Kris was on your mind. And he's our brother. He can never be forgotten."

I took two large swallows of wine. The restaurant was dim and quiet, with candles at every table. I stared at the flame until it hurt my eyes.

"Math, what's wrong with you? When I picked you up at the farm you were weird, too."

"I wasn't. Everything was fine."

"You seemed less than relaxed, that's all I'm saying. Feeling relief from the Burn should be a weight off, not on."

"It was just, you know, a chore. It was done."

"A chore? Not more than that?"

"No." I fiddled with my fork. I grabbed my napkin, unfolding it, then folding it up again. "Shouldn't it be better than just grabbing someone and having at them?" I realized my question came out a whisper.

Trigg leaned forward. His reply, simple. Straight-forward. "Yes."

"Hmm." I nodded.

"Not every Burn is great. Sure. Of course. And if you're keeping yourself distant. Or if you feel ashamed."

"I've never felt ashamed!" I said.

Trigg just blinked at me.

"I take what I want. Always. You know me. I have fun wherever and whenever I can." My voice came out a bit more defensive than I'd intended.

"You have changed."

"What?"

"I mean from when we were kids. You used to be funny, more carefree. We all looked forward to our eighteenth birthdays and our Burns. All of us. You bragged about your first time. You said it was so great. But after more Burns, after a couple years, you bragged in even colder more crass ways."

"I did not. Besides, we went to different schools. You weren't even around."

"Sure thing, bro. But you're a lot of bluster, you know that? And then a while back the bluster stopped. Like, maybe a year ago?"

"I have no clue what you're talking about." I was miffed at him for all this. Bringing up moods? When he didn't even hang out with me all that much? Didn't really know me? That wasn't fair.

"Math, I'm not a total stranger. We grew up together. I know you like I know myself. We had the same father, the same blunt-ass cold as ice father, and the things he put into our minds, well, each of us handled them differently, you, me and Kris. After Kris left, more and more I could see you trying to impress Father, be like him."

I started to interrupt him but he shook his head.

"You were. You wanted to be the favorite. I've always known that. And you achieved that. Father loves you. You're smart, you like money, you do everything he tells you to. It's okay, but you know something? You get to be you, too. It doesn't negate Father. And something *is* on your mind or you wouldn't have brought up Kris to Father. So spill."

I chewed on my lower lip. My throat started to go dry.

Trigg's eyebrows came together, an innocently worried look. "Is it so hard to talk to me? I'm your brother. I'm here and always have been. I got you, you know, even if you are a turd sometimes."

Trigg blinked.

A warmth came from behind my eyes, unusual, unwanted, rarely felt. My voice rasped as I blurted, "I can never mate-bond, you know."

Trigg took a drink of his wine, then tilted his head. "Says who?"

"Says me."

"Why?"

I took a deep breath. "You have to promise you will never tell another soul."

Trigg made the cross his heart gesture. I thought he might actually laugh, but instead he sat very still and waited, his face relaxed and intent on me.

I looked down at the tablecloth. "I have never—uh—I can't—uh—well, I don't knot."

The muscles around Trigg's eyes twitched. "I already know that. You told me you don't because you hate it. You don't want to. But wait... Never?"

"Never. I can't, I guess. Even if I try."

"You guess?"

I nodded. "Some Alpha I am, right?"

"Fuck that. So what does the doctor say?"

"What doctor?"

"You've never seen a doctor for this? Why not?"

"Why would I? I don't care, you know. It's not the end of the world. Fuck. Who cares? I'm an Alpha who can't knot. Big deal. There are people who are dying. Omegas who are sold—"

"Whoa, hold up there. Since when do you care about Omegas? Wow, I'm seeing a whole different side to my brother here." Trigg smiled. "And before you say another word, Math, babe, you gotta see a doctor. It could be something really minor and fixable. It's not your fault and it's not about being or not being the perfect Alpha."

"Isn't it?"

Trigg threw his head back and breathed out in frustration. "Gods, you're such an idiot."

"Asshole," I replied, raising my eyebrow to soften the name-calling.

At that very moment, the waiter came with our food. I folded my napkin in my lap and focused on what was on my plate. Chicken breast. Tortellini. White sauce.

I heard Trigg's fork scrape against his plate. I took a bite of food, noticing that Trigg was still poking at his.

"First things first," Trigg said. "A doctor. I can get you in to see my guy maybe even this afternoon. Will you agree to that?"

I hated this. I should have kept my mouth shut.

"Why you never told me before is--"

"Because it's no big deal," I interrupted, taking another bite. It looked good but I tasted nothing.

"All right. Will you agree to let me make an appointment for you? Or do you have your own doctor?"

I shook my head.

"I should have known. Father's regular planned check ups for us when we were kids made me hate doctors, too, but I have a good one. Okay?"

I grunted. I didn't want to go, but Trigg would never shut up if I said that aloud.

"Next thing. You brought up Kris's name. Just earlier you brought up Omega rights."

"I did not."

"You said something about bad things happening to Omegas. That is not how you were raised and I never heard you express a single concern about them, including about Kris. Until dinner at Father's. And just today. So obviously something's changed."

I kept eating. If my mouth was full, no words could come out, right? Then Trigg would be shit out of luck.

Trigg sat and watched me shovel in the food. I glanced up, noting the way his chin stuck out and his lips pursed when he was contemplating something. It was a look he'd had ever since I could remember.

"Stop acting like you can read me," I grumbled, and shoved more food in my mouth.

"But I can read you. Better than anyone. You and Kris. We shared a womb. We're litter-mates."

I gulped. "So?"

Trigg narrowed his eyes, half closing them, and almost glared. "What is going on in that dark and beady mind of yours?"

I rolled my eyes.

He slammed his hand on the table. "I've got it. You've met someone. Oh gods, not just someone. You've met an Omega. All this is coming up for you because you met someone!"

I stared back at him, unwavering. "Eat your food," I finally said.

"That's it, right? You met someone. Is it an Omega? Or maybe an Alpha, but you aren't the type to go for that. No, it's an Omega. You gotta spill. Tell me! How did you meet? Where did you meet? You have a thing for him, don't you? You do, I can tell."

"Shut up, Trigg. Just shut up."

He nodded, a smug smile on his face. "Confirmation. Your words. And you know I won't shut up about it."

"This was a mistake." I shouldn't have come. I didn't want to talk about Saber yet.

But Trigg was the only person in my life I trusted. He could keep secrets. He was my litter-mate. And he did know me. All too well.

"It's not a mistake, Math. It's a step in a direction I think you want to go. You just have to be brave enough to go there."

"What do you know? You aren't bonded, you don't have anyone steady, do you?"

"Not yet, no. But we're both young. It can happen any time. To anyone. Maybe not to everyone. Or maybe some Alphas aren't capable, like Father."

"I'm not capable. I told you that."

"Stupid idiot, you don't know until you ask a doctor. So that's settled. Besides, it's mostly up here, right?" Trigg pointed to his head. "The mate-bond is measured in blood, sure, but you gotta feel it. That's emotional. You might be a bit stunted there, bro, but you'll work it out."

Trigg was making a lot of fast assumptions.

"Why are you talking about mate-bonds? I never said I wanted to, just said I couldn't." I huffed.

"I know. But it's on your mind, right?"

I frowned.

"You never cared before," Trigg said. "So it wasn't a big deal. Now something has changed. And, well, I'm going to make an appointment with my doctor for you right now." He pulled out his phone and tapped several times.

"There. Done," he said. "3 p.m. I'll come by the bank and drive you."

"I can drive myself."

"You know what, dude? I'm coming with you. You can use some support. You don't have to do everything alone. You've been an ass for so long, right? Just stop. Stop."

I should have been offended. But he spoke the truth. It wasn't something I didn't already know about myself. I didn't care what he thought. I couldn't. But Trigg was a good guy. Always there for me even when I was a total buffoon. I appreciated it. He easily could have stopped speaking to me. Like Kris. Or rather, I cut off Kris, but same thing, basically.

"So it's settled. I'm driving you," Trigg stated.

I had stopped eating. Now I pushed my plate away. But finally, Trigg began to dig into his meal. As he ate, he peppered me with questions about who I'd met.

I grumbled. I grunted. I drank more wine.

By the end of lunch Trigg had excised from me Saber's name and that we had already spent one glorious night together. He was ecstatic. My brother. My litter-mate. The only true friend I had ever had through no fault of my own.

It was embarrassing. It was a huge relief. It was the weirdest lunch I'd ever had.

*

I couldn't stop thinking about Saber, about our night together.

Trigg picked me up for my three o'clock appointment right on time. Every step of the way I kept telling myself I would turn away. Leave. Not bother with a doctor or anyone else, and stay away from Saber and resume my life.

But things moved forward not of my own volition. Trigg got a parking space close to the office entrance. He came up alongside me, talking about some drafting project I had no ability to understand. And before I knew it I was inside, signing my name, filling out forms, showing my insurance card.

It took five minutes.

When I came out, Trigg had a huge smile on his face. "All done? Painless?"

I blinked as if waking from a dream. "He just needed a blood test. Said it would tell him what he needed to know and if I have to have more tests after that, they'll schedule them."

"And?"

"For now, I have a prescription. Simple hormones. I take one a day. I stop if I start to grow hair on my palms."

Trigg laughed. "Excellent. You're going to wonder why you didn't do this sooner."

"You know why," I said.

The smile dropped from his face and he took a deep breath. "Yeah."

Father had made sure all of us grew up with anxiety about doctors. Maybe he hadn't done it on purpose, but all the same, not a one of his sons liked them.

In the car, Trigg seemed to be his normal self. But I was not. I felt stupid, annoyed and grateful all at the same time. I turned to look at Trigg, who even at thirty still had the air of a boy about him, smiling, open, and innocent.

"Thank you."

Trigg glanced at me with a shrug. "No problem. That's what brothers do. Look out for each other."

I nodded, but my face grew hot. I had failed even at that. I had never looked out for Kris.

I stuttered as I asked, "If I—If I ever do decide to mate-bond with someone, how do you think Father will take it?"

"Math, we're not forbidden from that, you know."

"I know."

"Father will accept it."

"And if the Omega I choose has children by another man?"

"Hmm. Intriguing." Trigg winked at me. "You really have changed."

"Shut up."

"I think Father will have to accept it."

But if one of the children were an Omega? I did not say that last question out loud.

"Math," Trigg continued. "He does love you in his own way."

I said nothing because I wasn't sure. Father didn't love Kris anymore. It had been too easy for him to turn and despise him, as it had been for me. Alphas like me, like Father, we were not the exception. We were the norm. The world we lived in was on edge because of it, and we were so sure we were making the world better, keeping things in line.

But when I thought of Saber and how he was with his kids, I realized the big lie of it all. We Alphas weren't better. We never had been.

Chapter Eighteen

Saber

It was the longest day and my heart wanted to leap from its chest every time I thought of Mathias. I held my phone close to me. My body tingled. I had no appetite.

The longer I waited to text him, the more I lost my nerve.

Would I sleep alone tonight? I figured I would, but anticipating—hoping for more, I washed the sheets and made the bed. I cleaned the bathroom and shower. I set candles on the nightstands. I opened the windows to let in fresh air.

I wasn't thinking. The logistics of someone like Mathias ever returning here, to me, were impossible for my mind to sort. But still I worked, making a nest for us, feeding my fantasies. Yep, the hormones were in good order today.

While I was cleaning throughout the day, the boys said they wanted to help. So I gave them little dust rags and showed them how to wipe at flat surfaces. That lasted about five minutes before they dropped their rags and ran off again to play.

By dinnertime, I had energy to make soup and toast. The kids loved it, but I sat staring at my food and barely eating. The babes inside me felt like a heavy knot pressing my stomach, giving me the sensation I was already full.

Still no messages on my phone.

I put the boys to bed, reading them a story but never hearing the words. I hugged and kissed them both, holding onto them a little longer than usual until they both squealed, then laughed at myself on the way out of the room, admonishing them to "go to sleep now."

In the living room, I turned on the TV searching for something to watch. I leaned back, my arm over my head, and sighed. This was my life. It was fine. I loved my home and my boys. Everything was good.

Why did I want more? I had everything I could need. Drayden had never been around much anyway. And the house was mine, the way I wanted it. I was a very lucky Omega in so many ways. Many would think not because my mate had died, but I'd grieved him quickly. I'd worried more about the boys behind left behind than myself, but they had not known their Alpha father well, and they were so young. Their grief had been minimal.

I was a lucky one. My Alpha had provided. I had money. So many unwanted Omegas ended up living out their lives on chattel farms. When they grew too old to be desirable, to have their services sold, they took care of the younger ones, or became teachers, cooks, and maids for the young ones and the Omegas who did earn their keep. But here, I had freedom to come and go. I had it all.

But what I'd felt last night with Mathias—I couldn't forget it. That wonderful intimacy and all the emotions it wakened inside me gave me a glimpse of what could be. Of what I'd been missing all this time with only the bare bones of a bond with Drayden.

Now I'd had a taste and my body wanted more. *I* wanted more.

The memory settled in my mind like an obsession. It coursed in my veins and my heart, my cock hardening as the noise of the TV rippled unheard about me. I tried to settle myself more comfortably on the cushions.

The room seemed hot. Too hot. The air on my face fluttered like flame and the hair at my temples grew damp.

Mathias? Or the flu? Both options appeared menacing. Both made me feel like I was dying.

Running my hands through my hair, I pulled my feet up onto the couch and slumped on my side. A sound made me sit up fast. Alert.

A soft tap at the door had me standing. I glanced again at my phone. No texts. No messages. Nothing.

At the door, bare feet slapping the terracotta tile, I fantasized I could already smell him. Campfire on a slow fall wind. Distance of dire urgency. Tension like an approaching storm. Maybe it wasn't a fantasy.

I knew who it was. Still, I asked, "Who is it?"

"Mathias."

Yes. I couldn't open the door fast enough but in my haste managed to fumble the lock. I called out, "Just a sec."

I flung the door open a little too hard. Too eager. The world as I knew had misted over, spinning away. A new world stood before me in the form of a dark Alpha male, tall and regal, a bit glowering, and everything I wanted.

"Come in," I said quickly, a smile tugging the edges of my mouth.

"I don't mean to intrude." He sounded formal. Conflicted.

I couldn't help the small laugh that escaped my throat. "Uh, no. You're not intruding at all." I reached out.

My small gesture was all it took. Mathias stepped forward while I remained standing where I was and it caused us to nearly bump. Suddenly, his arms came up. I leaned in. My own hands pressed to his waist and the hug went from zero to fierce in one second flat.

I pressed my cheek to his chest, then raised my face and breathed in the expensive cologne of him at the crook of his shoulder, his neck. That was all it took. My eyelids fluttered. My cock hardened even more than it already was.

"You didn't text," I whispered. I scrunched my eyes shut as I instantly regretted my words. "Forget I even said that. You have a life. You owe me nothing."

Mathias tightened his arms. His chin slid across the top of my head. "I should have," he said softly.

Finally, he pulled back, hands on my shoulders. He wore a black suit with a white shirt, standard, but on him it looked anything but standard. His features were sharp, almost pinched as he narrowed his eyebrows.

"Where are the boys?" he asked.

"Asleep."

He nodded and his nostrils flared just a little, enough to tell me he was measuring his breaths.

I took one of his hands from my shoulder and clasped it, drawing him further into the house and kicking the front door shut with my foot.

He followed silently, his footfalls precise and quiet as we moved down the hallway, past my office and the boys' room, and into my bedroom.

I shut and locked the door, then let go of him and picked up the long lighter. I wandered about the room lighting every candle I had laid out. The room flickered to life like a beacon to us, a cozy retreat made of glowing light. When I turned to look at him, all the tiredness of the day drained as my blood began to hum at the sight of him.

He stood in the center of my room facing the bed, looking ominous except for the dawning light in his eyes as they met mine, an appreciation mixed with a little confusion, and unabashed desire.

I sat back on the foot of my bed and reached up to him.

He came toward me as I spread my legs and he stood between them looking down at me with that dark, sardonic gaze I could not get enough of. I might have first thought he looked *down* on me, mocked me with his seeming disregard, but now I saw more. So much more. How he'd been with my boys. How he'd made love to me— it was making love, not my imagination—last night.

He was hiding things. Unsure. Filled with secret pains. Realizing that, he wasn't scary at all. My boys had never seen that side of him. They had taken him as he was at face value from the moment they'd met him.

142

I only took a bit longer because I had been so annoyed at the forced financial guardianship, and the subsequent meeting at the bank. Mathias had been so cold and hard at first, so *superior.* I'd bristled. My first impression had caused me to despise him.

How quickly things had changed.

I closed my thighs around his knees and tugged him down to the bed on top of me. He went willingly, putting his hands on either side of my body to support himself so he didn't fall on me with all his weight.

Holding himself over me, he leaned down and kissed me, taking my mouth fully with his lips and tongue, licking his way inside me. I wrapped my arms around his waist, hugging so hard I pulled myself up from the mattress, clinging to him.

He shoved his arms beneath me and before his weight could settle fully over me, he pulled us both onto our sides so we faced each other and continued to kiss me.

I'd never been so turned on. He was broad and steely and intensely dour at times. So perfect.

I was thrilled to see our blind attraction was mutual, for as I scooted up further onto the bed we both began undoing each other's clothing—buttons, ties, zippers—tossing garments right and left until we pressed naked together. My mind spun in pleasure.

I couldn't believe my luck. Mathias had come back. My Alpha had returned and was once again in my bed.

My cock was so hard it almost hurt. The skin of my ass was wet and ready. Normally I needed extra lube for intercourse. It was like that for most Omegas. But with Mathias I hadn't needed any last night. And tonight looked to be about the same.

I was wet. I was ready.

He took his time caressing me and, like before, did not shy from my belly. He cupped my abdomen, running his fingers up and down it and around my belly button.

He let out a short breath. It almost sounded as if he said a word. It sounded like *mine.*

But of course that had to be my imagination. It was too early for Mathias to make any claims, and too early for me to even think it. Knowing his family line, I felt fairly certain he would never make a claim on babes who weren't his own.

Still, at just the thought that what I heard might be true, I arched up, my body quickening even more, so ready for him.

"Please," I said. I didn't want to beg, yet at this point I didn't care. "I'm ready. I want you inside me."

Most Alphas would take to fucking right then and there without being asked further, without checking to see if the path toward penetration truly was clear, slick and open.

Mathias did not. He tipped me onto my back and pushed his hand beneath me.

I pulled my legs up so he'd have easier access. He touched my buttocks, both of them, holding the cheeks in his palms, then ran his fingertips up and down my crack.

I groaned, lifting my hips up, encouraging him.

"You're so damn beautiful," he breathed.

My mind became light as air at the compliment. "So are you."

I reached between my legs to touch him at his center, right above where his hard cock stood away from his body, and the silver ring glowed at the base. His flat, taut stomach was like touching metal encased in flesh. He was so firm, the muscles as if carved from stone.

I ran my fingers over his cock, then grasped it. He let out a hiss. I felt him move closer, saw his dark head come up to meet my gaze in the candle-pulsed dark, eyes glowing, as I guided him to my opening.

The head of his cock met the slickness of my hole and my muscles pulsed against it. I felt myself open to him.

"Push," I instructed.

144

He gave a little flick of his hips and the tip was inside me, hot, swollen, demanding. He let out a harsh breath in pleasure.

I pushed forward and felt my wet channel suck him into me. The sensitive walls of my hole became instantly stimulated and I knew I was going to come internally, and fast.

"Fuck me," I whined. "Do it because I'm going to come. I'm going to come."

He thrust all the way in, then pulled out and thrust again.

He rocked into me with quick motions and before I knew it I was over the edge, my anal orgasm ripping through me from the base of my spine to the top of my head. My hard cock throbbed with the intensity, but didn't shoot yet.

Mathias was good. Really good. He kept thrusting hard, harder, taking me through my orgasm, wringing it out of me. He pumped his hips while leaning down to kiss me again and again.

I held my legs open, resting my feet against the sides of his hips, feeling my ass stretch for him, accept him. My cock slapped against the curve of my belly.

My grandest wish in this moment in time was that he would knot me.

When he came, he pulled me up to him, then turned us onto our sides and his cock slipped out of me leaving me feeling empty. He held me to him in an embrace I considered to be intimate.

He did not knot me.

*

Every night for two weeks, Mathias came to my house.

Sometimes the boys were already in bed, sometimes they were still up. He never ignored my boys. He always spoke to them as if they were people, not children.

Every night we ended up in my big, purple-draped bed with the candles lit and dancing golden shadows on the walls. Mathias stayed later and later with me, but always left before the sun came up. I was sure by now it was because he was being polite and not because he wanted to leave me.

But he never knotted me.

Usually, Alphas knotted during their Burns. That was a given. But they could also knot outside the Burn if circumstances were right, and if they had strong feelings for their partner.

Most especially it happened if a bond was beginning to form. Alphas could not resist attempts to grow the bond, or even finalize it, through knotting.

Drayden had knotted me often, including before we married, but the intimacy between us, instead of increasing with time, began to decay about a year after our marriage, degree by degree.

Maybe Mathias thought differently about such matters. Or maybe he didn't feel the same things I felt. Though in bed it didn't seem like it. He cupped my swelling belly in a proprietary and gentle manner. He made sure I was satisfied every time, both ways, giving me internal and external orgasms. At times he held me so tightly I almost couldn't breathe.

He told me I was beautiful.

We'd started to text. Finally. Little things throughout the day.

Me: *Do you like spaghetti? If so, drop by tonight in time for dinner.*

Mathias: *Do you like pizza? I can bring pizza so you don't have to cook.*

Me: *When you get here today, hopefully don't mind the mess. The boys have been spectacularly rambunctious today.*

Mathias: *Lunch with pompous asses, friends of my father. I miss you.*

These texts were, in their own way, also intimate by my definition. The one day Mathias said he missed me, my heart nearly shattered into a hundred pieces.

I had fallen for him, but I didn't dare say it to his face. By nature, he was not verbose, which to me meant he lived behind a lot of walls he'd built up over time. A hardened man could be the most sensitive when confronted. I feared I'd chase him away if I were too forceful.

But sometimes, after we'd orgasmed together a couple of times, and lay drowsy in each other's arms, we would speak.

Mathias asked me once, as if hinting toward more of a future between us, "When you were married, what did you do with the kids during your husband's Burns?"

I loved when he asked me personal questions. I wanted to be as open as I could with him. "Sometimes they went with my in-laws to stay a couple days. Or we'd hire a nanny and we'd get a hotel room."

"Oh."

I longed to ask him for a knot, but some instinct inside me held me back. And that silver cock-ring—it was always there.

I asked him about his brothers. He would talk about one called Trigg, but not about the other, though I knew he was called Kris.

"Trigg," he said, "is a far more decent human being than I am. He's stuck by me. Even when I don't deserve it."

"What makes you think you don't deserve it?" I asked.

Mathias tilted his head back on the pillow, his muscular arm still under my neck, his other hand palm down over my belly. "I told you. I'm not the good guy."

For a moment I kept my words to myself. This repeat confession came slow and awkward, and out my peripheral vision I saw him staring up at my ceiling unblinking.

In my experience growing up surrounded by people, by Omegas of all ages, when someone made a statement like that it was because they regretted some action. Usually it was something like lying, cheating, stealing. Or hurting another.

I turned in the bed to lay my head along his upper arm. His hand slid over my side and down to my hip, making my very spent cock throb. Damn, but I could not get enough of him.

I watched his flat, dark chest rise and fall, his brown nipples still hard from our enthusiastic lovemaking.

I reached out and ran my hand over his taut, curved pec. "I want you anyway," I said softly. "Despite that. Including that. All of you."

He took a few breaths. The last one came out in little bursts. "I'm not good at talking about stuff like this."

"I know."

"There are parts of me I don't think anyone could ever accept. You'd do best if you just let me go, forgot about me." Mathias started to sit up.

Of course he was blunt and distant and sharp. He'd said things without thinking first, especially when we'd met at the bank. About Tybor. Making his opinion about Omegas and their place in society quite firm from the start. In that moment I hadn't liked him at all. But something had happened when I'd reproached him. Maybe he was just a jerk, or maybe no one had ever stood up to him before. Maybe both. But when I told him Tybor was my child and I loved him, he'd gotten a look. I don't know what had entered his mind, but he'd backed down. He'd changed.

He was more attentive to Tybor than Luke. I couldn't believe it was all so he could get a piece of single dad ass.

"No!" I clung to him. "I accept all of you already. You can't stop me."

Mathias fell back into my arms and ran his lips up my jaw and cheek, kissing his way into my hair.

I rolled on top of him, smiling as I leaned down to kiss him. His mouth opened to me. He wasn't blocking me. He wanted me. Deeper than mere sex. I knew it. Could feel it to my core.

His hands roved up and down my back, cupping my ass, holding me close. I truly had fallen for him. I knew as he held me, stroking, that I loved him. It made me feel both weak and strong at the same time. I wondered what he thought, how he felt.

I couldn't get it out of my head that he'd never knotted me. I wasn't sure what that meant, but it concerned me. It could mean anything, but I was the type of guy to take it to heart and worry about it.

We dozed for a while in each other's embrace, made slow love again, and I could feel the low-lying but incomplete bond between us simmering. It was then I decided to take the initiative. I'd planned it in advance, but wasn't sure I was going to go through with it until this moment.

"You are over here every night, you know."

"Mm hum."

Tracing his soft, dark hair along his shoulder, I said, "It's a lot. So just in case you want to leave some stuff here, I cleaned out a drawer for you."

His body went very still. Finally, he said in a flat voice, "I'd have you over to my place but for the boys."

"I know. I understand that."

"Not that the boys wouldn't be welcomed," he added quickly.

"I know."

"I just thought it was easier on you for us to meet here."

"It is easier on me. And I'm fine with it, Mathias. Really, I am."

"Hmm." The way his voice went low made his chest vibrate against my cheek and ear.

"That's why I cleaned out a drawer. Just in case you want to. For your convenience."

Mathias sat up and I came up with him, putting my arm through his as we sat in the darkness, the pillows at our backs.

Finally, Mathias responded. "Thank you."

After we showered, I showed him the drawer.

He nodded. "Thanks," he said again.

I waited for more. Something more. Anything. My heart yearned to hear him tell me his feelings. His body told me quite clearly, but I was old-fashioned, too. I wanted words.

I went back to bed and Mathias got dressed and left a few minutes later.

I lay staring up into the dark for a long time, missing his presence with every cell in my body. It wasn't until the light of pre-dawn began to turn my window treatments a pinkish bronze that I finally fell asleep for a couple hours rest before the boys would be up and ready for breakfast.

Chapter Nineteen

Mathias

The empty drawer did not bother me, it thrilled me.

It spoke to me. Saber wanted me with him. He wanted me to be at his house every day, every night. He wanted me.

Of that I had no doubt. No. If I had any doubts they were within me, a deep-seated conviction that I was wrong, meaning something inside me was wrong in too many ways. I wasn't good enough for Saber and his little family. I would only be in the way. It might even be worse than that and I'd cause him harm. How could I know?

I didn't feel the way normal people felt. Didn't have the same responses. For me it *was* normal; the world I grew up in and came to know was very black and white, and harsh about how those sides played out.

Omega's rights? They were a nuisance and caused trouble. Omegas treated as breeding stock? What was wrong with that when that was what they were made to be? It was how their bodies worked.

All these thoughts and more, which Father had taught as facts to us boys growing up in his strict, no nonsense household never took into account individuals and their minds, hearts and bodies. Facts were facts. People had to face them.

I never saw Omegas as individuals, not really, and I was ashamed for that sometimes, but buried it. Until Saber. Until meeting his twins and looking into Tybor's innocent eyes.

He hadn't asked to be born Omega, and he and his brother's stunning need for love and acceptance from a warm and generous father was unexpected.

I simply hadn't seen it before. Or felt it. My own Alpha father did not participate much in our rearing. He hired people to do that for him. Hired them for all but giving the tenderness every child craves. For that we had only each other.

I had never known my Omega father and never would. I'd given it no extra thought or energy.

But now my whole foundation was shifting under my feet. Saber was shifting it, and I wasn't sure what to make of it.

The cleaned-out drawer meant everything to me. It was also a terrifying reminder of my flaws.

There was no denying a low-level bond linked us. I couldn't stand leaving Saber anymore. At work, as I did my small duties, I was distracted by thoughts of him. All day I watched the clock, counting the minutes until my body could touch his again, until we could connect.

I pictured him with the boys, laughing with them, cleaning up after them, wiping their tears, giving them hugs.

This father, this Omega, this man had done the same for me, in essence. He gave his body to me. His affection. The now empty drawer.

I was like a child with a new toy but I wasn't sure I completely understood it. And certainly, I wasn't worthy.

I couldn't even knot.

I'd taken my pills for over two weeks now. Nothing had happened.

A call to the doctor told me sometimes they took a while to bind to the system. The doctor had told me to give it another few weeks and after that, if nothing improved, he'd do more extensive tests.

I dreaded it. I put the pressure on myself to perform.

Saber was wonderful. Everything I desired. I was always hard for him. I could come inside him several times a night if we were so inclined. My orgasms ripped

152

through me until I saw stars. Not even during my Burns did I experience such intensity.

But no knot.

I read a few online articles that said stress and pressure from the Alpha to perform could contribute to WKS, a stupid acronym for "weak knot syndrome."

Father thought he was so proper and perfect and fine and pure. He thought he produced little pure-bred Alphas who were the best of the best, the smartest, the strongest, the most beautiful. But then came Kris, whose Omega parts were only discovered when he turned eighteen. He had every Alpha characteristic otherwise, including Burns, but atrophied organs for another sex.

And then there was me. The perfect big Alpha. Hell yeah, so rich and smart and wearing the best suits, colognes and hair gel big money could buy. And yet I couldn't knot. The most enviable of Alpha traits, the thing that helped create the purest, most healthy offspring—I couldn't do it.

If Father knew, he'd probably have ostracized me years ago. Or worse, made me swear to keep it a secret not because it was personal to me, but because if it got out it would shame the family name and hurt the businesses.

My face heated with shame. I practically heard Father's voice next to me as if he were in the room with me. "If you can't knot, you can't be a true Alpha."

Fuck that. Add to that, I didn't fucking have WKS. I didn't have weak knots. I had *no* knots. I wanted to throw my computer across the room of my office when I read that. I wanted to go somewhere dark and nameless and drink myself to death.

When I had these urges, I would flip back through Saber's texts to me, rereading how sweet they were, how encouraging. How loving. They would make me smile and I knew something had changed inside of me. It had been changing for a while now, but the final push had come from meeting Saber and his boys.

Saber had cleared a drawer for me. The final message that communicated to me was he wanted me to claim him. That was clear and inarguable. He wanted me to claim him as much as I wanted to.

But I couldn't.

How could I tell him I was so fucked up? I was not a great guy, but this on top of everything else felt ruinous to me.

Knowing Saber, he'd still say he wanted me anyway. It might even be true. But I didn't want myself. I didn't want to be this way. How could I accept even a partial mate-bond if I couldn't even accept myself?

The empty drawer. It said a lot. It opened up a lot of darknesses within me.

*

Trigg texted me.

Mathias, damn it, when can I meet him?

He'd been bugging me now for about a week. He wanted to take all of us, me, Saber and the boys to dinner one night. He wanted to see this incredible Omega who'd charmed the fucking pants off me.

Damned annoying.

But he kept at it until I said yes.

Saber had made me a clean drawer. Trigg wanted to take us all to dinner. Could my life be any weirder? Yet, I was giddy. Happy. I wanted to see Saber again. Right now. If going out with Trigg meant a short day at work and I could leave and go pick up Saber and the boys sooner, I'd do it.

I took a deep breath. I texted back.

You are annoying as hell. Let me check with Saber for tonight. I'll get right back to you.

I texted Saber.

Trigg wants to meet you.

Saber replied instantly, as if he'd been watching his phone more than his kids. He texted back within seconds.

I want to meet Trigg.

I texted him the time and place and added:

He wants to take us all to dinner. Kid safe. I'll pick you all up at five.

It was nice to shorten my day a bit. What work I did have was completed quickly and with utmost excellence. I knew the job. I knew finance. It was, simply, that Father gave me more in name than workload, as if he'd never really trusted me in the first place.

I left earlier than I needed in order to pick up some things on the way.

As I swung into Saber's driveway, I looked in my rearview to make sure the car seats for the boys were secure. From what I'd researched, five year olds still needed them, and I'd seen Saber use them in his own vehicle.

The white front door of the house flew open and the kids spilled out onto the walkway, jumping, skipping, running in circles, doing pretty much any form of ambulation but walking. Their pale hair fluttered against their necks and foreheads.

Just as I opened my car door, Saber walked out and my heart jolted to see him. Every cell in my body wakened, as if to call out to him. The sensation was like a fever, but not the Burn.

I stood with my door open and the boys came running.

Tybor yelled, "Hi!" and waved as he ran toward me. Without thinking, as he nearly ran into my legs, I caught him up and swung him into the air.

"How would you like to try out the new seats I got for my car?"

"New?" he asked.

I nodded, narrowing my brows.

"I wanna try," Luke cried.

Before Saber could approve, I had Tybor already into one of the back kid's seats and strapped in. Sitting by the seat I had two little toy wands, both made of clear plastic and filled with water and glitter. I handed him one.

"Tilt it back and forth and watch as all the colors tangle and spin," I said.

His eyes were big as he took the wand from me.

"It's a magic wand," I told him.

Next came Luke. By now, Saber was right behind me, watching as I settled his kids for the ride and gave them more toys.

"You have car seats," he commented.

"I do now," I replied.

"You got these just for them?"

I turned to see his face. It had been only a little over two weeks. It was perhaps presumptuous, but then again—

I said. "You emptied a drawer for me. This was the least I could do."

"You haven't put anything in it yet," Saber observed. But he was smiling, his bright hazel eyes filled with late afternoon light and something else swimming there, something like love. Maybe it was love. But what did I know of love?

"Not yet," I replied.

"You sure know how to keep them occupied," Saber said, indicating the boys who were tipping their water wands back and forth, staring at them in awe.

We got into the car and I drove us all to the restaurant.

On arrival, Trigg met us in the parking lot. He waved, smiling, and I wondered how it came to be that we had grown into such different people. Trigg was happy, open, generous, unafraid. I was everything the opposite.

"Good to see you big brother." He rarely called me that, though I had been the first born of our triplet-litter, with Kris coming second, and Trigg the last.

Trigg touched me briefly on the shoulder, but refrained from hugging me, for which I was grateful. He was the hugging type. He respected that I was not about fifty percent of the time.

"And you must be Saber," Trigg said.

The boys, having climbed from their car seats, stood one on each side of Saber, clutching their colorful, magic wands.

Saber reached out to shake Trigg's hand. "Nice to meet you."

Trigg bent down and looked from one twin to the other, and said, "And who are you?"

Each boy responded in turn, proudly giving Trigg their names.

Trigg shook their hands; they were awkward and amazed.

We all headed to the restaurant entrance. Trigg swiftly came up alongside me and spoke low and fast into my ear. "You didn't tell me he was pregnant!"

"Oh," I murmured. "Didn't I?"

Once indoors, we went to our table which had been reserved by Trigg. We sat, ordered drinks, and small talk ensured.

I let myself observe Saber with Trigg, watching for signs—of what, I didn't know. Anything. Whatever might let me know if each approved of the other.

I wasn't sure why I was worried. What did I care what Trigg might think? But Trigg was the one family member I trusted. Of course I would never tell him that. Not out loud.

I thought, then, of Father, how everything I did was about trying to be more like him. About how I idolized him. Admired him. But trust? No. I didn't trust Father. Not in the least. I never had. My personal life was nothing we ever discussed beyond amenities. It was all business with Father. All about appearances and being the best as Alphas in strength, looks and brains all wrapped in designer wear made for men of our stature.

"Math?" Trigg asked.

I came out of my thoughts and glanced up. "What?"

"You didn't tell me you're Saber's financial guardian."

"Oh, yeah. That was how we met."

"I didn't know you did that job at the bank."

"Normally, not. But I was filling in for a friend."

"Lucky for me," Saber said, grinning. "He got me a new mortgage that kicked hundreds off my monthly payment."

"I oughta be good for something," I replied, letting one corner of my mouth crook up.

Saber laughed. "Agreed."

Trigg just looked at us, his gaze going back and forth between our faces. Then he shrugged and said to Saber, "What can I say? My brother's always been a genius with money."

"What do you do?" Saber asked Trigg.

Trigg was off and running, fast-talking about his art teaching first, which was his passion, and then his design work. Saber kept up, though. He seemed very interested.

What I did for a living was dry in comparison. Sure, I crunched numbers. But mostly I kept up Father's front. I was part of his brand, a money brand, but somehow Trigg had managed to squeeze out of that deal and go into his own thing.

Did I have a thing?

And why was I thinking all these questions right now?

It was annoying, all these thoughts going through my head, so I turned my attention to the boys and commented on the puzzles they were solving on their kiddie placemats. It was a good distraction and they never asked me questions that were difficult or required me to probe deeply into my own psyche. What a relief.

Dinner went by quickly with good food and drinks. I was glad Saber and Trigg were getting along. Something about seeing my brother and my lover casually talking, smiling, laughing made a lot of the deeper worries inside me recede. If they were happy, then my own situation might not be too far off from the same. This was the logic I used, along with a couple beers, to help me relax.

On the way out of the restaurant, in the darkness of the parking lot, Trigg came up to me while Saber was helping the boys into their car seats.

"This one's a keeper," he said.

"We'll see."

"Why do you say that? I mean it. I can see the bond forming between you. Smell it."

"I don't know."

"You're not holding back because he's pregnant?" Trigg whispered.

"Gods no. Although Father would have a field day."

"Fuck Father," Trigg hissed. "Just—what about you? A ready-made family. You ready for that?"

I never thought I'd want to be. I didn't answer him. Also, what I said was true. Father would possibly disown me. That fact was not as simple as it sounded. Father and his ideas and his expectations were deeply ingrained in me.

"You need to be ready, Math, because if you fuck this up, you'll regret it forever. I can tell."

I grunted in response. It was all I would allow him at this moment because Saber was ready to go and now looking at both of us expectantly.

Trigg said, "I had a good time this evening," he said to Saber. "Such a pleasure meeting you!"

"Me, too!" Saber eyed me. "I didn't know Mathias would have such a charming brother. Maybe I picked the wrong one?" He winked at me.

Trigg laughed. "You," he said gesturing to Saber, "are much too sweet for this dour guy."

"Let's leave before this nice evening is ruined," I heard myself mumble. I held the door open for Saber, who slid into his seat. Then I walked around my car to the driver's side.

Trigg started to turn, but called over his shoulder, "I'm happy for you, brother."

"Thanks."

It did seem my life had taken a better turn. Why was I so hesitant to embrace it?

*

The boys were so sleepy when we arrived home, we each had to take one in our arms and carry them inside. For the first time since meeting Saber, I helped him with the ritual of putting the boys to bed. Usually, I waited for him in the living room or bedroom for him to complete that chore when I arrived at his house before their bedtime.

But now it felt natural to carry them into their bedroom. I had Tybor and I placed him on his stuff-animal piled bed, helping him off with his clothes and into his PJs which he proudly showed me had trains in a pattern all over them.

I turned to his pile of toys. "Do you sleep with each and every one?" I asked.

He shrugged and reached out to grab a plain brown bear which had been sitting next to the kitten I had given him. "I like this one best."

"Why?"

"My Alpha daddy gave it to me when I was little."

I almost chuckled at the word *little*, but realized he was looking rather grave and solemn.

160

I sensed Saber watching us, but I pretended not to notice. I said, "I think that's a very good reason to have that toy as a favorite."

Tybor took a deep breath, his eyes wide, his lashes glimmering as he looked up at me. Then he knelt up on the bed and put his arms around my waist. He could not reach all the way around me, but he did his best, hugging me as he put the side of his head against my belly.

I wasn't sure what to do. My hand went to his hair and petted.

"All right, boys," Saber said from behind me. "Into your beds."

"Do we get a story?"

"Not tonight. Dinner ran late. It's waaaaay past your bedtime. You need to go to sleep now, okay?"

Tybor leaned away from me and scrambled under his covers. I helped him pull them up, listening as Saber kissed Luke and tucked him in. Then Saber came to Tybor and did the same.

I backed up and watched. Luke was staring at me with big round eyes. "Good night, Luke," I said softly.

"Good night, Mathias," he replied.

The day I had told the boys to address me by my given name had thrilled them. They had been calling me *Mister* for days and I hated it. Now it felt just right when Luke said my name.

After we turned out their light and closed the bedroom door, Saber turned to me in the hall.

"Tybor hasn't brought up Drayden in months."

"Oh?"

"Thank you for helping me with their bedtime."

I stared down at him, then reached my arms up and brought him to me. "Your turn," I said.

Saber chuckled as I pulled him close. "You going to take care of me now?"

"I am."

In Saber's bedroom, Saber fell back onto his bed and stared up at me, grinning.

"One day," I said, standing over him as I took off my jacket and tie, "I'm having you over to my place. All of you. The kids, too. We'll put them in the guest room. They'll be fine."

"I'd love to see your place," he replied, shouldering out of his shirt.

"I have a pool. Don't worry. It's behind a locked gate. Do the boys swim?"

"Yes, they love to swim. They have been having lessons in summertime since they were three."

"Good."

When we were both naked, we fell together on his bed. His legs spread easily for me. He was wet and ready, his gorgeous cock standing straight up, swaying toward his firmly rounded belly. My own cock throbbed with arousal.

I didn't hurry, though. I never wanted to hurry with Saber, something inside me craving to take my time with him, to make him feel as good as I possibly could.

I ran my mouth over his nipples. My fingers stroked his soaked hole, and I stuck one inside him as I moved my head down to take his cock in my mouth and suck.

He grabbed the purple spread with both hands, his head arching back, showing me his pale throat. His hips shuddered, moving up and down as I played with him, and brought him to an orgasm with my mouth, his lovely cock shooting his pleasure into my mouth.

I was so thirsty for it. For him. All the time.

"Please," he begged, still breathing hard. "Come inside me."

I pushed his thighs back exposing his ready entrance, which gaped open for me now, and glistened in the low bedroom lighting.

Lining myself up, I breached him slowly, taking my time to make sure he was comfortable.

He tossed his head, grumbling. "Mathias, you're going to kill me."

It felt so good. It was hard for me to hold back, to not simply quick-push all the way into him and begin to thrust. I wanted to fuck him into the mattress. I wanted to claim him. Now and forever.

He didn't seem adverse to the idea, but I needed to take my time with him. He was pregnant. Vulnerable. Even a partial bond with an Alpha husband he had rarely seen when Drayden was alive needed time to heal, be put to rest.

Finally, I pushed all the way in.

"Move," he demanded.

I obeyed, thrusting in and out of him, holding his legs up at the crooks of his knees as I took my own pleasure.

He moaned loudly. "Harder," he hissed. "Faster."

His curved belly was firm and round and barely moved as I thrust harder.

He cried out. Obviously, he loved it. Something I was doing stimulated his sensitive Omega glands within.

"There," he said. "Yeah. Right there. You got it."

He started to hiss and groan more until I felt his muscles contract around me in his second orgasm, the internal kind that seemed to roll over his entire body.

That was it for me. His muscles milked me better than any hand, and his wet hole sucked at me, making me see stars. I came hard, pulsing into his heat.

He held himself open, letting me thrust through my orgasm in quick, little bursts of power and motion.

When I pulled out, my cock was gleaming with our combined juices, and still hard. I put my hand at the base of my cock, feeling around the ring, feeling hopeful for a knot. It seemed that this time, maybe something would happen. I'd come so intensely. My cock was still hard.

But there was no swelling at the base of my cock even when I unhooked the ring.

I looked down between us, as if my own intent could bring it into being. Nothing happened.

"Mathias?" Saber's voice flowed toward me through the shadows, through the quick breaths and the aftermath golden glow of our lovemaking.

When I didn't answer, Saber sat up, balancing on his arms.

"Mathias? Are you all right?"

"Yes." I leaned down over him. "You're wonderful. Everything."

"Are you—" He paused and gulped. "Are you holding back?"

"No." I felt horrible that he might think that. I deftly snapped the cock-ring back into place without him seeing.

Saber put his arms around me. "You don't have to, you know. The pregnancy hormones make me want it. And the stretching is good for the birth. You can't harm the babies. You don't need to—"

"I know that. You told me." I brought my body down beside him, my hand trailing over his stomach.

Saber leaned up on one elbow, turning to face me. He reached his free hand out and touched the hair at my temple. It was still in a tight braid, but some strands had loosened.

"When is your next Burn?" he asked quietly.

This was the first time he'd ever broached the subject with me. Something about the topic sent a shiver down the back of my neck. I didn't want to think about it. And yet, I did. I wanted to bond him, and that could only happen during a Burn. Yet not being able to knot made everything incomplete.

"Not for another month."

"I can take it. I can be here for you during. I just want you to know that. My increased hormones will accommodate it. Invite it."

When I didn't say anything, Saber added, "But only if you want. I just thought I'd say that, so you can choose. I mean, we've never talked about being exclusive."

"I don't want anyone else," I interrupted him.

"Good," came his soft response. "Me neither."

"It might come sooner."

"What?" He seemed confused.

"My Burn. It happens. I mean, because I'm taking hormones right now. It can affect it."

"You are?"

I nodded. My face was so hot right now. I didn't know what to say. I wanted him to know everything, but shame washed over me like a tidal wave.

Saber put his hand on my chest and pushed me until I was flat on my back. He sat further up in the bed until he could lean over me and place both his hands on my feverish face.

"Are you all right? That's all I need to know."

I nodded, looking up at his bright, intense gaze.

"Good. You aren't sick or anything?"

"No."

"That's a relief," he said. "Because I just found you and I want to keep you. You know that, right?"

"You do?" My words sounded pathetic, but honestly, I wasn't sure at this point what he really wanted.

"Of course I do."

What did I want? I wanted Saber. I had already proven to myself I couldn't be apart from him even for one night. Trigg had said he was a keeper. And Trigg tended to be right about a lot of things in life.

"You should have someone better."

"Better?" Saber asked.

"Someone good. An Alpha who is whole."

"What do you mean?"

Saber still had my face cupped in his palms. I tried to turn my head but he held it still.

"What do you mean *whole*?" Saber asked again.

It was all too much too fast. "Just that I'm not," I said, pulling away from him, from the sweetness, the salt of our sex, the lilac of his skin. I sat up with enough force that he fell back. Swinging my legs over the side of the bed, I made a grab for my strewn clothing.

"Hey, hey. Mathias. Wait. What are you doing?"

"Going," I said.

"I'm sorry if I asked too many questions."

I sat on the side of his bed, my body bent, and rubbed at the skin of my forehead. I was too uncomfortable in this moment. I needed to leave.

"I have an early appointment in the morning. I need to get home."

I heard silence from behind me. I didn't dare turn to look at him. If he seemed hurt, I wouldn't be able to bear it.

The world teetered. The world of the bedroom and Saber and his family. Why had I ever thought it might be a world where I could live?

I pulled on my pants and stood, fastening them, then bent and reached for my shirt. I heard breathing behind me, but otherwise the room was still. Still as held breath. Still as silent tears that might or might not be dripping down one of our faces.

It wasn't me. No, it wasn't me who went down the hallway to the front door, opening it and walking into the night alone. It wasn't me who pushed forward with each step, getting into my car and driving away. It was someone else. Someone who'd taken over my body and had been trying to be me for twelve years, since I first discovered the brother I thought was perfect was flawed, since my first Burn when I couldn't knot.

The next day, I called in sick to the bank. No one cared. There were no board meetings that day and I could work from home.

The little twinges of the new beginnings of a bond inside me, a bond with Saber, stung as I turned over in my bed, turned off my phone, and kept the room dark. I got up only for water and to use the bathroom.

It felt damn good to hide away from the outside for a little while.

Chapter Twenty

Saber

Mathias had never left so abruptly before after we'd made love. He'd simply walked away without even saying a goodbye.

I took deep, even breaths to calm myself as I heard his car pull out of the driveway and rumble off into the night.

It had been such a great evening. The dinner out. Meeting his brother Trigg. The time with the kids. Our coming together in passion as we did every night since the third day after we met had been perfect.

Now I was alone. Alone and sitting in my bed wondering what had just transpired.

I'd asked him too many questions, maybe. But only after he'd made cryptic statements that demanded more details. Not my fault. Something about him taking hormones and not being whole.

It was a problem for him, something big, something that triggered him to jump up from the bed and quickly run off. Leave me.

For a long time I sat in my bed amid all the heady fragrances of our heated love, my head in my hands, and regretted asking him anything about what he'd meant. I wasn't stupid. I knew he was reticent, private, found it difficult to show his emotions in the open. He had hidden shames. One concerned his brother Kris, though I didn't know the story there.

I should have been quiet. Let things rest. Let Mathias tell me whatever he wanted to say to me in his own time. Slow and methodical. Hesitant and secretive. It was his way and I didn't mind it. I didn't at all, as long as I could have him, keep him.

I kept replaying his words to me. *You should have someone better. Someone good. An Alpha who is whole.*

How could I tell him he was already everything to me, no matter what?

I touched my full belly where my new set of twins grew, wrestling more and more within me every day as if they couldn't wait to meet the outside world.

Mathias had never knotted me. But it wasn't for lack of wanting to fully claim the bond that was quickly forming between us. I knew that. He wanted me as much as I wanted him, or he wouldn't have been showing up on my doorstep every night. He wouldn't have bought car seats for his car. He wouldn't have invited me to his place and told me he had a pool and asked me if my boys knew how to swim.

I lay awake for a long time trying to understand. To make sense of him.

By morning, when the kids got up, I'd barely slept.

I tried texting him a simple *Good Morning* several times but determined my texts were not seen.

All day I brooded, trying not to show my mood to Tybor and Luke. It was a difficult day. I was in my sixth month of pregnancy and it was making me very tired.

That night, I checked my phone probably a hundred times. No texts.

I waited up past ten for Mathias to arrive, as he always did, on my doorstep. But by that late in the evening I knew it wasn't going to happen.

I went to bed more depressed than I'd been since Drayden had died leaving me and the boys alone.

The next day, I searched online and found Trigg Vandergale. He made it easy, didn't hide himself at all.

I messaged him.

Have you heard from Mathias? I haven't seen him since the night we all had dinner together. (And by the way, thank you again for a great evening.)

168

I checked the text over twice before sending it, making sure I showed no undue emotion. I didn't want to give much away. Mathias struck me as a private guy, even with his own brother, and I didn't want Trigg to set off some alarm.

I got an immediate reply.

I've been texting him with no answer. Not unusual for me not to get replies from him for as long as two days.

I replied.

Thank you.

But as soon as I hit *send*, another text came in from Trigg.

Not meaning to pry, but is this usual for you two?

I thought about lying. Telling him everything was fine. But it wasn't. I really was hurt. But more, I was worried about Mathias. I kept it simple.

No, it is not usual.

Trigg replied:

I can tell you're being protective. I'll check up on him. I won't tell him you texted, ok?

I actually nodded and smiled at my phone as I typed:

Thanx.

There was nothing more I could do. I had already sent numerous texts to Mathias. Another would be overkill.

If he wanted to break it off, I needed to know. It would hurt. But I would survive. No matter what, that's what I did for my family, my kids. Survive.

The partial bond between us had already formed threads of emotional links between us. Through them, I could feel him. Unlike with Drayden, where our bond was less emotional and more about convenience, I could feel that Mathias was alive. That much I knew to be true.

Also, underlying my own anxieties and yearning, was an aggravation that was not my own, and nothing to do with me being upset over my lover being absent from my bed for one night. This feeling—I wasn't sure what the exact emotion was, shame? guilt?—was definitely coming from him, not me.

It had all started when he admitted to me he was taking hormones and I asked him if he was okay. I didn't think my question invasive or upsetting. But how could I know what he thought in that moment about himself? If something was wrong, he had never hinted about it to me before.

As I heard the boys come in from the yard demanding lunch, I continued to stare at the phone, unmoving.

They came down the hall to the living room and found me, each one climbing into my lap.

I set my phone aside and held them close, kissing each on his forehead.

"Daddy," said Tybor, his little hand pressed gently to the top of my belly. "When is the babies coming?"

"A little while longer. Why? Are you eager to see them?"

He nodded. "It will be fun to play with them."

"Are you going to be the best big brother?"

"No!" Luke exclaimed to my left. "I will! I'll be the best!"

"I will!" Tybor argued.

"I know you both will." I leaned forward and they slid to the floor, letting me get up.

"Now, what do you want for lunch?"

"Peanut butter!" Tybor exclaimed.

"Chicken and stars!" Luke said, clapping his hands together.

"Hmm. Maybe we can have a little of both?"

"Yay!" They jumped up and down and ran ahead of me into the kitchen.

I glanced at my phone on the couch pillow and picked it up. No new texts.

My eyes misted over. I blinked away the dampness. *Mathias, damn you, I miss you.*

I saw him in my mind's eye, standing with his shirt undone, his flat abs exposed, his dark skin glowing. His head was turned away as if he couldn't look at me for some reason, as if he were gazing off at something over his shoulder that was distracting him, interrupting him, upsetting him. It made his demeanor even darker, and his emotional walls dense. The bond between us sparked and vibrated, but low-key and intermittent. I had to concentrate to feel and maintain it.

My boys called me, needing me. But what I needed? He wasn't responding. At least not right now.

Chapter Twenty-One

Mathias

As I approached the driveway where flowers in a dozen shades drifted and bobbed in a low breeze and the lawns were perfectly laid out and square cut in their emerald splendor, my heart skipped a beat.

The house stood in the middle of it all like a rectangular piece of cake, three stories, black and white with bright windows that shone in the afternoon sun.

When I reached the front door, it took me a long time before I pushed the button for the chime that alerted the household to a visitor.

I heard footsteps approaching from beyond the door. The golden handle rattled.

When the door opened, Reilly greeted me as expected, wearing his formal black suit with the tails and a jaunty red bow tie. He'd worked for Father since before I was born. More than thirty years.

"Mathias." His voice came cold as if forged from the interior of the home itself. "Is Master Vandergale expecting you?"

Reilly stood to the side in his high-handed polite way, as if graciously allowing me to enter the place that was my own fucking birth-home.

"No." I could compete with him and win in tone for cold and clipped if I wanted to. I moved briskly past him, almost but not quite brushing him with my shoulder.

"You might have to wait to see him, then. He's in his office. He's had a lot of meetings today, both in person and online."

Father had an arsenal of tactics. I knew them well. One of them was to pretend he was busier than he actually was so he could put people off, make them wait, which allowed time for them to over-think their positions and gave Father the upper hand. It worked pretty much every time.

Today, I'd deliberately *not* made an appointment. Taking a turn at Father's arsenal with the strategy of surprise, the one where you were not to give the other party time to prepare for a meeting, was one I loved to implement.

"You will tell him I'm here," I said to Reilly. "I'm sure he'll find time for his favorite Alpha son."

"Yes, sir." Obedient, but cool, Reilly was the sort of Alpha servant who became loyal to the job alone, and attached to one person. In this case it was to Father. It wasn't a romantic attachment, though the notion caused me some amusement—thinking of Father who was such an Alpha's Alpha lying with another Alpha—but I was sure that would never, ever be the case.

Maybe I myself was a little like Reilly. Attached to Father. Loyal. But it was different. I was his son. Reilly was not.

I stood in the vast living room of the manor, taking in all the details that were as familiar to me as my own hands. Certain things brought back childhood memories, such as the heavily cushioned couch by the side window where Kris used to sit for long hours and read. The old chess set in the corner made of onyx and white marble where Trigg and I played many, many games to the death.

This area was also the last place I'd ever seen Kris. It was the place where I'd said more horrible things to him. I'd called him flawed and believed it. I'd told him he wasn't a real Alpha. I'd hated him because when Father had been impaired by the Burn, Kris had enticed him. Or so I believed.

Now I had some years on me, and a whole lot of perspective. Trigg and his constant talk, never minding that I didn't want to hear half it when he updated me on Kris and Thorne and their bonding, had slowly sunk in. I knew better now. I knew I'd judged Kris wrongly. That I had threatened him with rape and said things no brother should ever say to another.

But back then, I'd followed in Father's footsteps so closely, I didn't care who I hurt to retain my position. That need to be Father's best son blinded me.

I had believed, because of Father, that Kris was trouble and a terrible influence on Father, taking advantage of Father's deep love for him, and that Father couldn't see straight when he was around him. It was wrong. I was wrong. I knew that now. But so many years had passed I couldn't see any way to make up for it.

All of this was fucked up. And then into the bank walked Saber. I didn't deserve him and I knew it. All of this was so fucked up, and now I'd walked out on him.

My phone the past two days had become filled with unanswered texts from Saber and Trigg. I didn't know what to say. I didn't know what to do.

That was one of the reasons I stood here now, in Father's house, in my old home. I had to see him. I had to talk to him from my current perspective. Be sure. I had to know. What would Father say to me if I announced I wanted to marry an Omega with children?

It came down to this. I needed to see. To be sure. This insanity all these years concerning Kris, my own shames, and Father's weird ideas about mate-bonds, Omega children, and Omegas as merely chattel, wasn't my own thinking. My own original belief.

It stemmed from Father himself. Sure, some of it was cultural. But the rejection of Omegas, the despising of them, including when one presented Omega who was your own son, that was the insanity that maybe, just maybe took things too far.

I heard Reilly come back down the winding, marble steps.

"He will text you when he's ready for you," Reilly reported.

174

I had to curb my instinct to push past Reilly and mount the stairs, run up to Father's business study and pound my way in. Why did he use his tactics on me?

Again, there I was, thinking I was too good for Father to treat me as anything other than his perfect son. And feeling incensed when I didn't measure up.

I would wait. I would be fine about it. I wouldn't let it affect me. I told myself these things, but I barely believed them. Not anymore.

"There's a sofa in the hall outside his office. I'll wait there."

Reilly gave me a disapproving look but said nothing. He knew what was best for him. Never to argue with Varian Vandergale himself. And also not to argue with his son.

I took the stairs slowly, holding my phone so I could feel the vibration of it when Father was ready to see me. I had just reached the closed door of Father's study when the phone buzzed in my hand.

Knocking on the door as I opened it, as I was taught, I stepped inside the large room. A hearth took up the far left wall. It was a warm day out, so no fire burned there, but when one did, the flickering light and heat would fill the room and give off a luxurious, cozy feel.

A determination and strength filled my chest—until I saw Father sitting at his desk as if too busy to pay any mind to me.

This was another of his strategies. Even with his own sons. With me. He would always make us wait just a little longer for the attention we craved from him, even when we were very small.

Finally, after tapping on his computer keyboard for a few seconds, tilting his head at his screen, then straightening some notes at the side of his desk, he turned toward me.

"Mathias!" He stood and came toward me, taking me into a familial perfunctory hug. I touched him once with my open palms on his back, then stepped away.

"You're looking great! What brings you here in the middle of the day—and without an appointment?" he asked.

I didn't feel like taking my time, or hedging around my reasons for being here. I got straight to the point.

"Father, I'd like to inform you so you don't wonder where I am that I'm taking a personal family leave from the bank. I believe the law says I can do this for up to six months."

"Six months? Why? Isn't your ample vacation time sufficient? You have six weeks a year. That's more than generous. And you realize personal family leave is only for Alpha's who have pregnant bondmates."

"I do realize that."

"Then the answer is no. You already have a high salary job for very little work. The hours you put in are already leisurely."

"I assure you I have been in attendance full time." It never bothered me much if Father thought I was lazy. In truth, I was. But I was also smart and what work did come my way got done fast with utmost efficiency.

"Still, I need you there. Your name and your face. You can take some weeks off, but not six months. That's my final word."

"You don't get a final word in this, Father."

"Excuse me?"

"There is someone."

He tilted his head making me hesitate and I hated myself for it.

"Someone?" he asked.

"In my life. Someone I hope to bond with."

"Are you dating an Omega?"

I nodded, my mouth going dry. "I am. And I intend to make a claim. He is pregnant, thus the family leave time."

Father spread his hands and a smile bloomed upon his face. "You are to have a child? Why am I only now just hearing about this?"

I swallowed hard. "Two children already exist. Two more are on the way."

"What? How? What are you saying, Mathias? You are a father and you never let me know it?"

"I wasn't. I mean, I'm not. I mean, the children are another Alpha's, but--"

"Hold on. What are you saying? You are having children? Or are you not?"

"Father, just listen for one moment."

He got that hardened look about his features I had despised and emulated at the same time since I was five years old. "I'm listening."

"I met him at the bank. It involved a financial guardianship. His name is Saber and--"

"You met an Omega at the bank?"

"Father, please. Just let me speak." I took a deep breath. "Saber was widowed several months ago. He has two small children from that marriage. And two more on the way. I met him at the bank and things went from there. The beginnings of a bond formed between us. I am still unsure about many things, and perhaps I'm not the best mate-bond material, but if he'll have me, I intend to make a legal claim to the bond, then ask him to marry me."

Father held up his hand. "This all sounds rash to me. Even crazy. Did this Omega coerce you in any way?"

My eyes widened. "Of course not, Father."

"You're not behaving like yourself. You barge in here. You insist on time off. And you say you're not the best for mate-bonding when anyone in the world would stand in line to hook you into their lifestyle. You see that, don't you? That your name and money make you ripe and open for being used. You've avoided it thus far, your private dealings never becoming personal, but what has happened this time?"

"What has happened, Father, is that I want him. I want *him*. And his family will become mine once we marry."

"Which is foolish at the very best, my son. Don't you see?"

I blinked hard. I'd expected this. His blind spot was when things became imperfect, not in line with his expectations and thinking. He became unbending and annoyed. Even paranoid.

"At any rate," I continued as if he had not spoken his insulting opinion, "I will be putting in for family leave. My mate is entering his third trimester and I will need to be there for him. After he gives birth, we'll need time to assimilate the household to the new twin boys. I'm here to inform you of this fact."

Father's face turned soft and hard at the same time, if possible, his eyes wide but his mouth a firm line. "It's outrageous, though. Don't you see it?"

"I didn't come for your approval or your blessing. But I didn't want to inform you through email, either. That's why I'm here today."

For a moment, Father looked stricken. As if he'd been betrayed. Then he turned abruptly and went to his desk. He leaned over it and straightened some papers. He put his hand on the back of his desk chair and remained like that with his back to me.

It was awkward as hell in this room, now, but he didn't care. I don't know what had made him this way in life. Hell, it was my unquestioning admiration of the man who made me what I was. Maybe his own father had been just as cold and demanding, and Varian Vandergale had learned it from him. I'd never met my grandfather, but I could imagine him as a cold, hard Alpha just his son.

Finally, he spoke. "You are not obligated to raise another Alpha's children," said Father. "If you like this Omega, you will still like him in a few years when his children are grown and on their own. Then you can produce your own offspring with him. The prudent thing to do would be to wait."

This was Father at his best, his way of compromise. Showing his favorite son a willingness to accept him but on his own terms. That was another strategy to his dealings. It made him good at business. But, I only now just realized, he rather sucked at raising kids.

"No." I spoke just the one word, nothing more.

"No?"

"No," I repeated. I didn't want to wait. Saber's eyes, his strident voice, his lilac scent—they all called to me. He was alone. He had two babies. And two more on the way. Every instinct in me defied my reason and my preference for being independent, unchained. I wanted to help him. The urge was to provide and protect. Protect that family and make sure they all had everything they might ever need.

I loved Saber. That was a fact. One of those things Trigg always said was a part of life and you could do nothing about it but deal with it. Trigg had a long list of those things. Most of them I ignored. But this time, the word on his list called *love* was something I was no longer capable of dismissing. The callous cad I used to be had been snared. And hell, I didn't really mind. Not now. Not standing here in Father's study in a house that cost more than most people made in a lifetime.

Father stared at me as if I'd grown horns. The word *no* seemed to echo about the room.

"You will do what you want to do. You always have." Father said it like it wasn't quite a compliment.

"I simply wanted you to know. From me. And not have to wonder."

Father's face remained neutral. "I hope you're not making a mistake," he said flatly.

Mistake? This? "I've made a lot of mistakes, Father. This doesn't feel like one of them."

"You?" He sniffed. "You've done impeccably well in life."

"One of the children is an Omega," I blurted. I'm not sure why I said it. I was testing him. Sensing.

Father's nostrils twitched. He sat at his desk and stared at his computer screen as if I had never walked into the room.

"Have you ever just thought about getting a dog?"

"What?" I tried to comprehend this statement.

Father brushed me off with a wave of his hand. "Never mind. You were an extreme child so much of the time. I cannot be surprised at this." He turned to look at me with half-lidded eyes.

"A dog, Father? That's your solution to avoid a mate-bond I want?"

"I'm very busy, Mathias. Thank you for telling me. You have your six months. After that time, you will have a job to come back to, but it might be a very different description."

That was Father's threat. I'd expected worse. I could live with it. But the awkwardness that was now between us? The family gatherings? Those would be worse. I would, of course, avoid them. If I never introduced Saber to Father, it wouldn't be much of a loss.

Something inside me lightened at the thought. The heaviness I'd felt walking into my childhood home lifted. I turned as if walking on air and left his office, closing the door behind me with a gentle push. Not a bang as I'd envisioned at first. Not angry in the least.

Chapter Twenty-Two

Saber

The TV kept the kids occupied for now. Late afternoon light streamed through the big windows, and the shadows on the back lawn were growing longer.

I sat at the dining room table, watching my silent phone for Trigg's texts. Trigg had already found out Mathias hadn't been to work the day after he'd left my bed so abruptly. Today had been another long day not hearing from him.

My phone chirped.

Trigg: *I went by his house and he's not there.*

My heart fell. Of course my mind went to all the bad case scenarios. Mathias had not only run away from me, but from everything. Just left it all behind. Or perhaps he was injured and hurt somewhere and couldn't get help. Or the worst of the worst: he was dead.

But why would he run? Just because he thought he wasn't whole? What did that even mean?

Me: *Does he do things like this? Run off?*

Trigg: *Never. Mathias doesn't run away from anything.*

Words which, of course, did little to comfort me. I sat for a long time trying not to think anything bad. Trying to blank my mind and listen to the titters of my children in the living room and just remain calm.

A few minutes went by with me focusing on keeping my breathing even, my eyes closed.

The phone chirped.

Trigg: *Last resort. I called my father. He saw Mathias not ten minutes ago at his home office. As is in my father's nature, he would give me no details of their meeting, though I did ask.*

I took a deep breath and let it out slowly. I knew he wasn't dead. Of course I could still feel the residual tendrils of our bond, a lacy warmth that shimmered through me whenever I thought his name or pictured him in my mind. But this confirmation was more welcome than Trigg could ever know. I'd had a small bond with Drayden and never felt his death. Calling this a relief was an understatement.

Me: *Thank you. His messages still go unanswered?*

Trigg: *Afraid so. But I'm going to try him one more time. Give me a few minutes?*

Me: *Of course.*

Five long minutes passed. Then my phone rang. It was Trigg's number.

"Trigg?"

"Yes," said the calm voice on the other end of the line. "I know where he is. So, uh, we have a brother named Kris. Did you know that?"

"Yes. He has mentioned that they don't speak."

"Yeah. Uh, do you think I could come by and pick you up?"

"I have the boys."

"Oh."

"I can try to get a sitter. I have one who's very good. Maybe he can come at the last minute."

"Try." Trigg's voice sounded insistent. "Call me back."

I had a good sitter I trusted named Caleb on standby but hadn't needed him in quite some time. Luckily, he answered immediately.

With the kids situated, I called Trigg back.

"I'm ready."

"I'm already on my way."

Chapter Twenty-Three

Mathias

The little two story house with the red shed sat behind a poppy-covered rise at the side of the road. For a long time I sat at the end of the drive with my car running, just staring at it. For twelve years Kris had lived there with his Alpha bondmate, Thorne.

Kris, my litter-mate. My brother who presented as an Omega at the age of eighteen and rocked Father's household in a way that had me smug and insanely jealous at the same time. So much so that I wanted to crush him.

What Alpha isn't an immature little shit at eighteen?

I remembered good times. I had tried to put them all out of my mind, but that was impossible

Kris and I used to sneak out of Father's house when we were kids and play catch with a ball in the cool, crisp grass of the estate. Trigg was more studious of the three of us, always reading, always drawing. But Kris and I were mischief-makers together. We hid from our tutors. We stole food from the cooks and left our dirty dishes and clothing and toys everywhere for the staff to pick up. We were brats together.

When we were ten, we stole money from Father's petty cash safe—breaking into it was no small feat—and put the bills in with the personal effects of the servants we hated. It got them fired and Father never found out they were innocent and that we'd played a nasty trick.

One time we constructed elaborate rope ladders to swing out our bedroom windows at night. We never used them. Where would we run to? We had no friends but each other. But we did it to make Father think we were sneaking out. He had a fit and punished us—making us eat dinner alone in our rooms for a week, such a hardship—but he also fired more servants for not keeping a better eye on us.

What Kris and I were doing was messing with the household simply to get Father's attention. When we finally had it, we competed for his favoritism, often trying to one-up each other. It was fun when we were younger. It became more serious the closer we came to having our first Burns.

But one night very close to our birthday, before our yearly exam by the old Alpha doctor Kris liked to call Doctor Pokeme, Kris started bragging a little too much. He said he swore he could feel his knot starting to form and he was going to mature into a tough Alpha, he just knew it. I was mortified. I hadn't felt anything near to what he was describing, but of course I lied and said I had the same experience, and I was going to go to the chattel farm when my Burn hit and have the time of my life.

It bothered me more than I would consciously admit to myself. Soon after, Kris was diagnosed as Omega and right around that same time I faced my first Burn.

Father had been horrible to Kris, locking him away. At first I was both glad and sympathetic. I thought maybe Father would simply fix the problem—like with surgery or something—and everything would be the way it had been.

But Kris remained a prisoner and my Burn hit. I had the fever hard. I couldn't think straight. I couldn't see. My cock hurt more than it felt good.

My first time, though the Omega was experienced and did everything right, didn't go well for me. I came too fast. Or I had trouble coming. It seemed like a never ending series of me being a stupid Alpha boy. On top of that, I had looked forward to finally knotting. I wanted to feel it. I wanted to know firsthand the incredible sensations we Alpha boys were all taught would shake us to our cores.

It never happened. I never knotted. The Omega never commented about it, but I noticed. I noticed every time. I tried to make myself feel it, to understand that maybe I was holding back because I was virginal and young. Still, nothing.

I told no one about it after my Burn.

I went home and bragged about how good my Burn experience was to Father and Trigg, who both seemed truly happy for me.

But inside, I was seething. Kris, who was an Alpha with atrophied Omega parts, had said he could feel his knot forming. He wasn't even a full Alpha and he was still better than me!

I hated him. When he attacked Father I didn't listen or care that it might have been in self-defense. I saw only his beauty, and his ethereal honey scent that had possessed him once he'd hit maturity, and I felt my Alpha self bristle to aggressiveness. Putting Kris in his place was all I could think about.

So I vented. I told him he was no one, unworthy, an Omega who was nothing but a hole now. A hole that was meant for Alphas, and nothing beyond that mattered. I told him I could rape him and it wouldn't matter. That I could have him and no one would care. That honey scent of him. It got me. Combined with the aggression I felt, it made me hard, for which I blamed him all the way. Blamed him in my thoughts, memories and dreams for years after. That his beauty and his Omega nature and scent made me shamefully want him? That was all on him.

My words crushed him.

Now I sat and looked at the house where he now lived quite happily according to Trigg, and the memories came on strong, making my heart beat fast until the ache was so pronounced I began to rub my fingers against the muscles of my chest.

My rage twelve years later still sparked red when I thought of the incident that had finalized the break between us. But that rage was so much less. And for what reason did I feel it? Kris had done nothing. It was my own mad stupid teenage hormones out of control.

I was no more whole of an Alpha than Kris. Father liked to think of us as his perfect, purebred Alpha sons. Kris had disappointed him, through no fault of his own. And all this time I myself functioned flawed and unwhole, an Alpha unable to knot. To do what Alphas did and carry on the seed to Omega chattel or mates, either way, that wasn't going to be me.

Three weeks ago the doctor had given me hormones. But he told me they only might work to help me knot. Beyond that, he could do nothing about the fact that my condition, after twelve years, had predisposed me to being infertile.

Doctor Pokeme all those years ago had said he'd checked that part of our Alpha status on all three of us. Were all Father's sons fertile? Turns out, Kris and I, his pride and joy and trouble-makers galore, were not. But he'd either been mistaken about me, or lied when he'd told Father I was virile and ready for my first Burn. In truth, Trigg was the purest Alpha of all of us. And he was the one who fucking didn't care.

Head down, eyes closed, all the memories played out in my head over and over.

A sudden pounding on my passenger side window made me jerk my head up to see a face peering at me, a surprised look on a man more beautiful than my mind ever imagined him now at age thirty. His voice came muffled.

"Mathias?" More tapping. "What are you doing here? You're blocking our driveway."

I quickly flicked the switch to roll down the window of my Ferrari. I said one word. Just his name. "Kris."

"Mathias? Are you okay?" He pulled at the door handle but it was locked. "What's wrong?" He looked down, his hand going into the car to find the button on the panel to unlock the door.

I heard a click.

The door opened and he came into the car, the door still open, and sat, turning halfway to face me. His honey scent filled my vehicle.

"Mathias? Is it Trigg? Is it Father?"

I shook my head. I had to keep looking straight ahead because if I didn't, if I looked at him, I thought maybe my mind would disintegrate into a million pieces.

"I'm sorry." I heard my voice as if it came from far away.

"What?"

"I'm sorry. That's all. Can you get out of my car now?" I put my hand on the steering wheel.

Kris stayed put. "That's why you're sitting out here all alone? Blocking my driveway? So you could say that? What's happened to you?"

"Nothing. I'll get out of your way now," I replied.

"I hated you at first. I don't anymore." His voice was low and beautiful as he spoke. Pure Alpha.

Why did I ever think he was otherwise because of a few atrophied organs? Trigg even told me he experienced Burns. I heard Kris take a deep breath.

"Mathias, I'm glad you came by. I really am."

"Fine." The word sounded weak. Pathetic. "I'll go now."

"I want you to tell me you're okay first. That you're okay to drive."

"I'm okay." What I really needed right now was a drink. Or six.

"I'm not sure about that. Why don't you come inside for a few minutes? I can make you some coffee."

"I'm fine," I repeated. I started the engine. "Get out."

"Come on. Just pull on up into the driveway," he suggested.

"No. I'm going now." My teeth gritted. I put the car into *drive.*

"All right. All right." Kris slid from the seat until his feet were on the ground.

188

The door bumped him in the shoulder, then closed. He started to lean into the window to say something else, but I pulled away, eyes on the highway, focused straight ahead.

I didn't remember driving. All I knew was I was sitting in the parking lot of a bar. The lights on the door spelled *OPEN*.

I got out. Behind me, a pick up pulled in and parked beside my car.

I could smell him again. Honeysuckle and sandalwood and a distinct Alpha musk.

Kris had followed me.

I no longer cared. I kept going into the bar, in the dark and the shadows. The first thing I did was order a Vodka. I leaned on the bar top and sucked it down, ordering another. Then another.

After that, I lost all track of time.

Chapter Twenty-Four

Saber

"There!" I saw Mathias's Ferrari in the bar's lot before we drove in.

Trigg looked where I was pointing and pulled into a space alongside it.

"That's Thorne's truck," he said, indicating the pickup on the other side. "He's Kris's bondmate and husband."

On the drive, which took about fifteen minutes, Trigg told me about Kris's call informing him that Mathias and he had spoken, and then Mathias had quickly driven away.

Worried, Kris followed him.

Now Trigg texted Kris we had arrived. He looked at his phone, then up at me. "Kris says he's been keeping an eye on him. He's had four vodkas and shows no sign of stopping."

"Maybe I should hold back."

Trigg frowned. "If anyone can reason with the guy, it's you. He's never had anyone like you before in his life."

"It's a free country. At least for Alphas. If he wants to drink the night away, he can."

I was scared. Maybe Mathias didn't want to be confronted. Maybe it would only make things worse between us. Yet I could feel the bond between us. What was there was vibrant and alive. His drunken confusion leaked through. Despair and anger and resentment. But none of it defined him. None of it was the true essence of the man who'd tucked my little Omega boy into bed, who'd placed his palm gently against my swollen belly and kissed my forehead, who'd made love to me until I saw stars.

Trigg nodded. "He can." He put his hand on my shoulder. "But we're also allowed to let him know we have his back."

"You've been that for him, haven't you? The guy who watches his back."

Trigg shrugged. "He's said and done things I don't like, but we have an understanding."

I nodded. "He's your litter-mate."

"He's my brother." He gripped my shoulder a little harder. "And you're coming in with me. We're going to meet Kris."

"Mathias might not be ready for me to."

"He introduced you to me. He let me take you and your little family to dinner. Mathias did not give that okay lightly. Possibly you don't realize he's never done that before. Never."

My breath caught.

"He's ready. Saber, he's been waiting for you his whole life, don't you see that?"

I blinked hard, feeling the hope in my chest spread. It was almost like pain.

We walked into the low-lit establishment. Some sort of jangly music played in the background, nothing I recognized. But then, I never hung out in bars. Ever. The music I was used to sang about 1-2-3s and ABCs and how to spell Bingo.

I really needed to get out more.

Trigg and I were immediately met by a tall, muscular Alpha who resembled Mathias in many ways, except instead of a dark braid holding back his long hair, his braid was blond. He was shockingly beautiful, though not as handsome as Mathias—in my humble opinion.

The blond Alpha and Trigg touched hands, exchanging slightly pained looks, then he turned to me.

"Hi. My name's Kris. Nice to meet you." Kris held out his hand.

I shook it, a light clasp, feeling the warmth of him, the gentleness.

"I'm Saber."

A honeyed scent washed over me like nothing I'd ever smelled off an Alpha before. I could tell something was different about him, but had no clue beyond that instinct.

I didn't have to ask where Mathias was. My eyes were immediately drawn to the hunched, dark Alpha at the bar, elbows on the counter, head down. I had to hold myself back from immediately rushing to him.

Kris looked from me to Trigg. "He knows I'm here. But now there're three of us."

"I don't want him to think we're ganging up on him," Trigg said.

"As I said, he showed up in my driveway unannounced," Kris explained. "When I came out to the car, he told me he was sorry and then drove away. He didn't seem right, so I followed him."

Trigg's eyebrows shot up in surprise. "He told you he was sorry?"

Kris shrugged and nodded.

"Wow," said Trigg.

"I don't know if I should even be here. I want to make sure he's okay, but if he doesn't want to see me--" I said. Air huffed from my lungs too fast.

Trigg put a hand on my upper arm. "You should be here. If he didn't care, he wouldn't be behaving like this. I'll go talk to him."

Kris and I both agreed.

I watched Trigg move to a barstool alongside Mathias, wave to the bartender, then turn toward him. For a few minutes, I could see him talking to Mathias, whose shoulders got tighter and tighter.

Kris and I sat at a table by the door, nervously watching. The notched wood of the tabletop bit into my elbows. I had my hands clasped in front of my chest and realized they were shaking.

Finally, Trigg and Mathias turned toward us at the same time. They got up. Mathias teetered a little, but Trigg caught his arm and they made it to our table.

When they came up alongside us, Trigg said, "Mathias would like Saber to take him home."

Mathias wouldn't meet my eyes, but he gave a quick nod.

A huge weight lifted from my chest. "I can do that."

What I really wanted to do was hold him to me as close as I could, and sink my face into his hair.

Mathias said, a little slurred, "You didn't have to come." Then he got a worried look. "Where are the boys?"

"They're fine. They're with a sitter."

Mathias turned to Kris. "You didn't have to come, either."

"Wanted to make sure you were safe, that's all," Kris said.

Mathias closed his eyes tight for a moment, breathing in. "Thank you."

"Maybe you would like some coffee before we go?" I asked Mathias.

He nodded.

I scooted over on the bench and made room for him to sit. Kris rose at that point, and he and Trigg stood side by side, watching.

Trigg said, "If you're sure you can get him home--"

"Thank you, yes," I replied.

"We'll go then. Mathias, call if you need us."

He nodded.

Kris leaned forward, his blond braid sliding over his shoulder. "Your apology is very much accepted, Mathias."

"You owe me nothing."

"Nonetheless," said Kris. "It is. I thank you for coming by today. And I like your new bondmate."

Mathias seemed to bristle at the words, but Kris just shrugged and gave a little smile.

Trigg elbowed Kris in the side, shaking his head.

Kris said softly, "Well, it's so obvious, isn't it?"

Was it? I was proud if Mathias would have me, but we still had to get through this evening. Together.

Kris and Trigg left and then it was just Mathias and me.

I sat with him for over an hour while the bartender plied us with coffee. Mathias still wasn't talking, so I took up the slack and spoke softly about the kids, their recent antics, and how they kept me on my toes.

"I missed you," I said softly, more than once. Possibly more than three times. I said it so he would know. No matter what. If he walked away or if he stayed. I said it so he would know.

"I want to come home with you but I don't want the boys to see me this way."

"Well," I said, "you seem pretty sober right now." I indicated the line of empty coffee cups on the edge of the table.

He shifted on the bench, his hands going to his pockets and pulling out his key lock. "Will you drive?"

"Of course."

When we arrived at my house it was past dinnertime, but I knew the kids would still be up. I pulled into the driveway, shutting off the engine. Neither of us got out right away.

I sat very still, imagining I could hear my heartbeat echoing off the car windows. I'd never wanted someone so much and been so afraid at the same time. I feared if I made one wrong move I could lose Mathias forever.

His voice came sharp and sudden. "I want to claim you."

For a moment, I thought I was dreaming. I swiveled toward him, mouth open.

He turned and his brown eyes met mine, glistening with an emotion somewhere between love and desperation. "But I can't. I can't bond."

"What? Yes! Of course you can. I want it. I want it more than anything."

"No. I can't. You don't understand."

I reached out to him. He flinched but allowed my touch, my hand settling on the front of his shoulder. "You can. We already have a bond forming. Can't you feel it? You can claim me, Mathias. I consent."

He gave me a pained little smile. "I do feel it. But I'm not sure it can go any further."

"Why, Mathias? Why not?"

His eyes closed.

My hand on his shoulder gripped hard. "Tell me."

He let out a few short breaths from his nose. Almost a whimper.

I leaned my head into him, sliding my hand from shoulder to chest, resting my forehead against the side of his face. "Tell me," I repeated.

"To fully form and consummate our bond, I would have to knot you."

"Uh, all right, then."

"No. You don't understand. I can't. I can't knot."

I swallowed hard, my mind spinning, trying to put together all the pieces of these last weeks, his behavior sometimes in bed, his silver cock-ring, his abrupt disappearance after he'd told me he wasn't whole. "Y—you can't. Uh, okay."

"And if you won't have me, I'll understand."

"What? Why wouldn't I have you?" He smelled of coffee, vodka, and strangely, the faint Alpha Burn of campfires. But he couldn't be approaching his Burn. He told me it was over a month away.

Then I remembered him saying he was taking hormones and they might disrupt his cycle.

"Is that why you're taking hormones?" I asked.

He nodded.

"Hmm. Well, you know what?" I rubbed my cheek against his jaw. "It's not a deal-breaker, you know. Knotting. It's not a make or break issue with me. We already have a bond forming. We can make a legal claim. You know we can. And you know I want it. With you. Don't you?"

"I do," he said softly. "But you deserve the whole deal. Not me."

"Fuck your whole deal thing. What is that anyway? You're everything to me. I want only you."

After a moment, he raised his hand to my face, pulling my chin up until he could touch his lips to mine.

Between us the bond flared in a way I'd never experienced before with Drayden, or imagined it could feel with anyone. A window flung open, it was like sliding into the star stuff of which my lover was made. It was summer and silver fire, safety and warm beds. It was shadow and sunlight and desire made of every beautiful dream I could recall, filling up my future with promises of more. It was as if nothing else mattered but this, and it was explosive.

When we pulled apart, I said breathlessly, "I want you. I want you with me for the rest of my life."

"I do, too," he replied, and in the dimness of the house lights I could see the beginning of his smile.

"Just don't run away from me again. Promise."

"I promise."

When we went inside, the boys came running and Tybor and Luke each crashed into my thighs, wrapping their arms around me. Then Tybor turned toward Mathias, looking up at him with big eyes.

"You came back," he said.

"Yes," said Mathias.

Tybor broke from me and ran to Mathias, wrapping his arms around his thigh.

At the same moment, Mathias bent down and placed his hands under Tybor's shoulders, lifting him up.

Tybor gave a little squeal of delight as he was swung up through the air. I watched Mathias bring the wiggling child close to his face and kiss him on the top of his forehead.

He held him close, and Tybor wrapped his arms around his neck.

"Did you think I could ever stay away from you?" Mathias asked Tybor.

My Omega boy giggled in the big Alpha's arms, and said, as if he were the wisest person in the whole wide world, "No. I knew you'd come home."

Chapter Twenty-Five

Mathias

In the darkness, in the softness of Saber's bed, he held me close, running his hands all over my face and into my hair.

The vodka I'd had—which had been a lot—was still not all the way out of my system. My mouth was dry. My mind careened at inopportune moments. I was more highly emotional than I ever remembered being in my life.

Through our bond, Saber was like a calm, easy, safe space. His mere presence was an embrace. His emotions were sane and sure, like guiding lights dispersing the shadows I'd surrounded myself with for more than a decade.

I never had any idea this was what a mate-bond could be like, even the mere beginnings of one.

He didn't do anything more than hold me and caress me through my clothing, and let me lie there and tell him things. Secret things. Stuff I had never told another soul.

He listened intently as I spoke of Father. Of my jealousies. Of my shames. I talked to him about Trigg. And then of Kris. And how my skin burned when I spoke of my brother whom I had neglected for so long. I told him what Kris had gone through, how Father had attacked him for being different, and how Thorne had found him hiding in his shed on a frozen winter night.

Trigg had kept me up to date on Kris's life. I was ashamed I had not kept up myself.

Saber said softly, "You judge the eighteen year old boy you were but forget the man you have become. That's everything. And I'm glad, so glad you're in my life now."

He let me grow quiet when it was too much. He let me take my time when my throat became too thick to speak further, or when I could not breathe.

After several long hours, we dozed together in each other's arms, the covers askew, our shirts and trousers half-unbuttoned. The intimacy between us felt nearly as close as if we'd just made love. Maybe even closer.

The bond licked my mind with warm streams of light. I floated on it and never had I felt more relaxed.

When the morning light leaked through the edges of the curtains, it didn't bother me. For I realized today I didn't have to do a gods damned thing. I could sleep in. I could stay with Saber all day and just bask in his home and his family.

I had six months before I had to go back to work.

In the early dawn, as the shadows turned a dusty rose, I pulled my sleeping lover close, and smiled.

*

The white pill looked innocuous, small and shaped like a barely budding leaf. The day was bright, shining into the dining room with a bit of a glare. The sounds of the boys laughing and playing outside lent a peacefulness to the house.

Saber had gone off to take a shower. I was keeping an eye on things.

I didn't mind at all. In fact, I enjoyed it. I would never have thought it of myself.

I stared at the pill. To take it or not. I had been taking them for three weeks now, and noticed no difference. The doctor told me it might be at least two weeks more before I would see results of the added Alpha hormones. I was getting impatient.

Saber and I had already made our legal claim upon one another at the mate-bond offices, complete with blood tests to prove the birth of our bond. We had documents of approval now. Things had moved quickly for us. But the final step, which I had been taught was necessary to complete a bond, was the knotting during an Alpha's first Burn with his chosen one.

That was something I couldn't do.

Saber came into the dining room, his hair still wet and slicked back, wearing a white pullover cotton shirt and jeans. His belly was somewhat hidden by the looseness of his shirt but the jeans rode low, and I could see the bump of his pregnancy when he moved, though he carried toward his back.

Seeing him full like that, entering his third trimester, and glowing from the shower sent waves of pleasure to the base of my spine, and tingles to my balls. My cock twitched with never ending lust for my bondmate. But deeper than that, my love for him washed over me in a flood of sensation and light and scent, along with sound like distant echoing laughter in my mind.

Saber sat facing me, hands on the table, and glanced down at the pill.

"You worry too much," he said.

"I want to be whole for you. Truly Alpha." It sounded stupid when I said it out loud.

"Mathias, you're everything I ever dreamed of in my deepest fantasies. If you don't know that by now, then I don't know what else to do."

He always said the right words. Always. What I needed to hear. Did I do the same for him?

"Do you not think our claim is valid?" Saber softly asked.

"I know it is."

"And how do you feel about that?"

"You're mine. Everything about you inside and out. Everything!"

Saber laughed. "The way you say that. Such conviction! But I'm not your possession. It's more than that."

"No," I agreed. "You're not a possession. But I think I might want to be yours. In that way. In every way." I flicked at the pill. "But this holds me back."

Saber leaned forward, his eyes sparkling. "Let your Burn come. The first one for us as a couple. Then we'll see. You want me to own you?" He grinned, showing white teeth. "You'll have trust me."

I nodded, picked up the pill and popped it into my mouth.

*

"Something is working within your body if it's come a month early," Saber said, handing me a chilled glass of tea overflowing with ice.

I sat in our bedroom against an array of soft pillows. Heat trickled up and down my arms and legs. Telltale signs of the Burn, along with decreased appetite, loss of focus, and an erection that wouldn't quit.

"The boys are safely off with their grandparents, who were thrilled to take them for a few days," Saber said softly, the mattress denting as he sat at my side. "They're so excited. They'll be going to Wonderland, and after that, the beach. Their grandparents love to spoil them."

"I'm glad they're happy," I said, straining to keep my voice even.

So many thoughts ran through my head. I wanted this time with Saber to be special, but I barely had control. I wanted to feel more than I had in the past, where my Burns had become shameful chores, just something to get out of my system.

I had only ever used chattel farms for my Burns. If I had sex between fevers, I used anonymous Omegas, the ones who were more wild or addicted to drugs. The sex meant nothing to me. The Omegas were non-entities.

I hadn't realized, until Saber, how cut off I'd been from myself, my emotions, the world.

Now it felt as if too much mattered and one wrong step might spell disaster. I had everything now. And everything to lose.

I drank half the iced tea down, then leaned back, holding the glass against my thigh.

Saber reached out and ran his fingertips across my brow. "Do you trust me?" he asked.

Of course I did. I sent affirmation through our bond, then closed my eyes and nodded, letting myself feel nothing but his fingertips against my skin. His hand brushed against my thigh, got hold of the cool glass and took it away. I heard a tiny clink as he set it on the nightstand.

"Those jeans look incredible on you, but they've got to go," Saber said.

His hands moved to my waistband.

I hadn't been going to work—a nice reprieve—and had taken to wearing jeans and casual pullover shirts about the house. I was used to being in suits and ties all day long. Every day. I had worried I'd be out of my element, but being with Saber and the kids I actually felt less encumbered. Freer.

Our bond gave me a place to be, to rest. To hold onto something other than jaded boredom and the stress of living up to the Vandergale name. Everything in my life pre-Saber had been about appearance, reputation, pride, all fueled by resentment, shame and anger. Being an Alpha came with a lot of privilege but also a lot of bullshit baggage. Being a Vandergale Alpha was even worse.

Saber was speaking now, softly, his voice stroking itself about my flesh, my heart, my mind. "Two hearts. Two minds. Though we are different people, split by different needs, with separate memories, Alpha and Omega, we consent to share a single union and destiny."

He was quoting the ancient marriage words. I knew them by heart. Every human being on the planet did even if they never married, or never had a ceremony.

202

He ran his hands under my shirt, gently pulling it up.

"Together we enter the Burn."

I lifted my arms and he tossed the shirt away. His hands came down hot over my chest.

"My beautiful Alpha," he whispered, trailing his fingertips over my ribs and the ripples of muscle below. "I love you more than life itself, for you are life and soul, a part of me now, never to be parted, I claim you."

His hands went to my waistband, undoing it.

I was hot, my vision blurry, but the words came to me not because I'd memorized them, but because I felt them born from deep within. Ancient and abiding.

"My heart, my soul, I claim you. Saber." I reached up to him. "I—I love you."

A low, happy chuckle escaped him.

"We enter the Burn together," he repeated. "I'm ready."

"I am ready."

He tugged at my jeans and my hips lifted to help as he teased them down my thighs, along with my underwear. My hard cock bobbed free and up, already wet at the tip, smacking gently against my belly.

Saber leaned down and ran his tongue all the way up the underside. The flames on my skin grew even hotter. I groaned, throwing my hand over my eyes, then peeking at him from underneath my forearm.

He grinned up at me. "I promise not to tease you too much, but damn, you are so delectable. Gorgeous."

"You can tease me. I—I love it. Because it's you and I trust you. I love it." I decided I was babbling. I decided I didn't care.

"Good, because I'm here for you. I want you every way I can have you."

He leaned down again and suckled the tip of my fully erect cock. Pleasure swirled through me, hot and hotter, the urge to thrust nearly impossible to contain.

One of Saber's hands went to the base of my cock and squeezed, giving me some reprieve, though very little.

Earlier in the day, on his suggestion which had come more like a command, I'd removed the silver cock-ring I always wore. It had been a form of protection for me. A way to hide. I felt incredibly bare without it.

Saber began to softly press his fingertips against the naked base of my cock, massaging, easing up, then pressing tighter again. His hands drifted about my pubic area, pressing, rubbing, massaging, as he kept sucking. The tip of my cock came out of his mouth, naked and shiny and round, the foreskin pulled all the way back now. No one but Saber had ever given me such beautifully detailed attention in that area.

He breathed upon it. "I can't wait for you to be inside me."

My cock twitched, though his ministrations at the base never let up.

I lifted my arm and my head. "What are you doing? It's incredible."

"Just trying something. No worries. Lie back. I'll mount you in a minute, you feisty Alpha."

"You need to be readied first," I argued. My mind moved sluggishly, but the Burn hadn't hit full on yet. I would take care of him. I wanted to.

"I readied myself," he said.

Finally, he took his hands away and sat back, butt against his heels, and lifted his own shirt off in one, smooth motion.

His gleaming fawn-toned body—the flat chest with the enlarged, sweet-pink nipples of pregnancy, the slight showing of his ribs as he stretched, the firm, convex curvature of his hairless belly, the low-slung jeans that pressed his lovely hip-bones and revealed the top curves of his perfect ass as he came up onto his knees and began undoing his zipper—all made me crazy with lust and love.

To know I was claiming this man, and he unto me, sent the room spinning. I blinked hard to still it because I wanted to watch. To fixate on him as he dragged his pants down and revealed himself fully to me.

He pulled them down with ease and lifted one knee, then the other to get the garment fully off his body.

His pretty, pink cock rose straight up, pointing toward the ceiling. He turned slightly and I could see the shine between his cheeks, already wet for me, wanting me.

My hands came up. I wanted to pull him to me, absorb him, take him.

He came willingly into my embrace, his nude body over mine, our cocks meeting, our chests, our chins, our lips.

He pulled back a little after a long, deep kiss and said breathily, "If you hold back, if you can let me, I want this first union to be about you but with me tending to your every need. But if you need to just mount me and go to town, that's okay, too." He laughed as he kissed me to let me know he was ready in every way.

"I want you to do what you want with me," I said. "While I can still think and see. I want you to tease me. I told you, with you and only you, I love it."

"Lie back and just enjoy, then, okay? I want to try some stuff, and I want you to trust me and I want you to relax. Tell me again that you can."

Gods, I loved him so much. Never in my life did I ever think I would be in this position.

"I trust you," I said.

"Close your eyes, and let me be everything to you. Feel me through the bond, and let it ripple between us."

I sighed and focused on letting my body go limp. But my raging cock made it difficult, coursing hormones throughout my system that trembled me, and made my muscles jump and twitch, primed for action.

I concentrated on our bond, still not fully formed, but strong enough to allow me to flow into Saber's brilliant heat and light, to feel his love without hindrance, without barriers. For a single moment, I worried about my shadows within, my memory so tangled with the good and the bad, but realized I wasn't alone. Saber had dark places as well, and guilts mixed in with good times and bad.

We were the same, just two humans trying to find their way in a world that wasn't fair. But Saber taught me it could still be a beautiful place if you knew where and how to look. If you met the right person or had the right moment.

This was one of those moments.

Saber's fingers massaged me up and down my thighs and my knees bent in pleasure. Everything was sensation now. I rocked with it, eyes still closed.

A tongue teased the tip of my cock, then ran all along the underside, lapping and licking and wetting. It delved to my balls where lips kissed and sucked at the sensitive skin there.

Finally, he took me into his mouth, softly at first, then harder, and I became lost in light, in him, basking in waves of open emotion through our bond.

I sank into the pleasure and love which seized me wholly, and I no longer had the need to buck or take, but merely float.

Saber's hands ran up and down my stomach and chest. One hand circled the base of my cock and massaged and milked. He let me slide out of his mouth and I kept my eyes closed as I trusted him to make the next move.

He moved up my body, kissing, licking. He pushed my thighs down and climbed over me, straddling my hips. He placed one hand over my heart. The other held my cock straight up, firm fingers surrounding the shaft as he lowered himself.

The tip nuzzled between his cheeks. It slipped a little; he was so slick. But he held me tight and guided me to his entrance, lowering himself onto me. My cock slid into his stretched and ready entrance and he moaned, taking me in deeper, his muscles tight but prepared to let me glide all the way in.

When he was fully seated, he put both his hands on my chest and began to move his hips.

To be fucked like this, with no strain on my part, no difficulty, no aggression, was like being claimed by my Omega, and I loved it.

He rocked upon me, his internal muscles milking my length perfectly. The Burn rolled over my flesh like a breeze of hot air, lifting, sinking, then lifting again with the rhythm Saber set. It did not overtake me in a frenzy of near painful desperation, but instead guided me higher and higher to ecstasy which I could feel echoing back at me within our bond.

My sensitive cock throbbed, the cells from the tip to the base blooming with the swell of more and more pleasure.

"I'm going to come." It might have been a whisper. It might have been a yell.

Saber quickened his pace, and his muscles squeezed me as he moved up and down my length. His own cock bounced up and down, tapping my belly, balls rubbing against my groin.

I groaned and all the colors upon the darkness behind my eyes went red.

The bond between us flared.

At the moment I crested, I felt Saber reached behind himself and between my legs. First he palmed my balls, which had tightened hard against my body, then he used his fingers to encircle my cock at the base, milking me there as well as with his anal muscles.

I shot hard into him, my fingers gripping the purple bedcover. My eyes snapped open. It was such a huge throb I couldn't contain myself. I sat partway up, lifting my hips to his.

His fingers kept milking and as I pumped more semen into him, his cock twitched and dribbled as he, too, shuddered and came, spraying a few shots over my chest. Yelling my name.

In that moment, everything that he was, and that was any part of him became mine to protect and love. Tybor. Luke. The twins waiting to be born. The territory of his house. The map of his entire body. I wanted to swallow all that affection and need, overwhelmed by my yearning to save, protect, open, claim.

Saber continued to move up and down my shaft with his body as I continued to spurt. I could not recall ever coming so hard and so much.

I almost thought I could hear him through our bond: *Come on, give it all to me. I want it all. I want all of you. Mathias!*

The slick warmth of him. The sweetness of his fingers tight around my base. His other hand pressing to my chest just over my heart. The curve of his stomach was so enticing, I put my hands there just to feel him, to encompass all that he was, and my shoulders and head fell back to the pillows.

Suddenly, it felt as if his fingers were pushing alongside my still throbbing cock and into him, all around me, surrounding me. It was the weirdest sensation.

Then I heard him shout. "Yes!"

My fingers splayed over his full belly, and I thought of the babes within, curled and sleeping, waiting for their moment in the future to join our little family.

More of Saber's fingers teased my cock at the base, pushing inside me. I wondered how he was doing this; he had to be twisted most uncomfortably.

When I looked up at him, his shoulders were straight. He sat on me, his hands at his sides, his hips rocking, his eyes glazed and glowing.

"What--" I began.

"Knot me, my Alpha, my bondmate, my love." As he spoke, he sank down hard on my cock. I felt his hole widen to accommodate—what?—my knot?

As the swelling grew firmer and firmer against the rim of his ass, I realized this was something different for me. Something new.

He was taking this thickness into him, his hole stretching to form around it and lock us together.

My knot. I was forming a knot and the pleasure of it felt like his fingers gripping, milking, pulling, only it was all me.

The knot sent sensations up and down my shaft, like continuous little orgasms all building to swell at the base and slowly move up the length.

I could feel the tip of my cock continuing to spurt.

If I didn't come apart and die right now from the ecstasy, I decided nothing in this world could kill me.

"Saber, oh gods, Saber!"

Saber rocked me with his ass and put his arms around my shoulders, holding me tight. "Lock me to you. Lock us together. I want it. I want to be mated by you. I want to feel your knot again and again and again."

My knees bent and my thighs came up to support him as he stayed in place, my cock with my knot inside him. I held onto his waist now, as if to keep him still. But he wasn't going anywhere, my Omega. He was staying right here with me, wanting me, needing me as much as I needed him.

The pleasure became so intense, my fingers dug into the sides of his hips, but he didn't seem to mind.

Saber threw his head back and cried out as his ass throbbed against my knot, pulling and tugging with his incredible internal orgasm. His hard cock shot more streams of white fluid which fell like burning drops of rain to my chest.

I fell back in ecstasy.

I felt it when my knot moved within him, like a throbbing, churning orgasm that never let up. Though I wasn't moving, it was as if I were thrusting in and out of him in frantic need.

Knees bent, my upper body came up off the bed again and I grabbed him all the way around his back, holding him tight to my chest.

Saber let his head fall to the crook of my neck, his hot breath burning underneath my jaw.

Our embrace tightened as our bodies remained stuck together.

"It keeps coming, the pleasure just keeps on and on," I said, my lips against the top of his head.

"I love it. Keep marking me. Keep coming, Mathias. Until you're done, and then we'll do it all over again."

Again? I would do this forever if I could.

He whispered against my neck. "Mark me. Claim me. All over. I make you mine. Make me yours."

"Within and without," I answered.

Through the bond I felt his pleasure build again, saw the two babes within him ying and yang, one Alpha, one Omega, and they too were bonding to us, their fathers, their parents, the ones who would love them and keep them safe as soon as they came into this world.

"We're yours," I heard him cry. Then he came again, milking more come from me, my knot surging upward at the friction, the stimulation, until it put so much pressure on the tip of my cock that I erupted with the greatest orgasm, squirting long and hard.

My balls quaked with pleasure. My spine surged with it. I went blind for a moment. Probably, I passed out for a few seconds as my cock exploded into him.

Later, he brought us water, lots of water, and vanilla ice cream in sparkling crystal dishes.

Then we did it again. And again.

I lost count of how many times I knotted him. I forgot I was in the Burn. Our lovemaking was so intense, and I was encased in so much affection and desire, that the idea of the Burn and needing to sate my rutting instincts never occurred to me.

Of course we were fucking, but it was so much more. I wasn't worried about getting it over with, or coming and leaving soon after with no feeling for it at all save cooling the fever of my body and my cock.

But now, with Saber, everything was about the two of us together, and that was all that mattered.

I locked to him in all different positions. He loved it when I held him from behind, both of us on our sides, and me rocking into him and locking us that way. I loved it when I could crouch over him face to face, and lock us up so we could kiss through the long, long minutes of ecstasy.

By the end of my Burn, we probably used every towel in the house. We took tons of showers. We laughed together like I never dreamed of doing with another.

When we became ravenous, we ate whatever we could find in the kitchen, wandering out there naked, stuffing our faces with more ice cream, bricks of cheese, apples, bananas, orange juice, lunch meats slapped on fresh slices of bread.

But mostly, we were interested in each other. Not food. Not showers. Simply, we wondered how fast we could get back in the bed and join together again, lock up again. We wondered how much more we could take before we rubbed each other raw.

Turns out, it was a lot. And when my Burn ended, we slept for twelve hours straight, arms tight around each other, legs tangled.

When we woke, we realized we could feel each other as intimately as touch.

Our bond had fully formed. It was complete.

Epilog

Saber

The lights were too bright, the pain in my gut intense.

Mathias, wearing black jeans and a black button up shirt with the sleeves rolled up his forearms, glowered with his arms crossed over his chest. He stood close to the side of my hospital bed as if he were my bodyguard. It would have been hilarious if I hadn't been in labor with twins.

As it was, he could glower all he wanted. In tune through our bond, he could feel echoes of what I was going through. He was doing his best to absorb the glory mixed with trauma of birth I'd already been through once.

He did everything I asked of him: closing blinds against the glaring noon light, grabbing more pillows to stuff under my chest, feeding me ice chips, anything he could do to make me more comfortable.

Most Omegas I knew, including myself, were most comfortable giving birth on their hands and knees. When the crucial moment came, I found it most comfortable if the bed was positioned in an upright position, my knees spread like a frog's, my arms clutching a couple of soft, spring-breeze scented pillows.

But right now, the ice was not enough to quench my thirst. Even covered by a hospital gown, I felt overly exposed. And the room smelled of too much antiseptic.

"Mathias." I turned my head toward him and held out my hand. "Come here."

He moved toward the head of the bed and took my hand.

"Closer." I moaned as a contraction hit me and made my body strain, all my muscles convulsing against my will.

He moved until his thighs touched the edge of the mattress, letting me squeeze his hand as hard as I could.

When the contraction finally passed, I inched my shoulders and head closer to him, and breathed in deep. He smelled of candlelight, of smoky autumn dusks mixed with a bit of my lilac shampoo which he stole every morning, dutifully replacing it when it ran out.

"You're a genius," I said.

"What?" he asked.

"You. How you smell. It's so calming."

He smiled down at me. His free hand rubbed circles on my back.

My first time giving birth, I had done it alone. Drayden had had to work. I couldn't be happier my second time was with someone who supported me and truly loved me.

Everything was damp between my legs, or padded. Or both. Another contraction hit. It hurt. It stretched me beyond what I thought I was capable of.

I heard the doctor come in. He spoke to me from behind. "Well, Saber, how are we doing?"

The contractions were rapidly coming one after the other now.

"We are ready to push these guys out now!" I squeezed out the words through gritted teeth.

Mathias kept hold of my hand and continued to pet my back.

I felt the doctor lift my gown and probe me with gentle, gloved fingers.

"I think you're ready now. I'm going to ask you to push. It will be soon, I promise, and then this will be all over."

"Fuck yes!"

Mathias patted me on my back.

"You go on doing that for him," the doctor instructed Mathias. "A little lower. It will help."

Mathias's hands were like magic, his touch instantly soothing as he circled around and around my lower back.

"Push now," the doctor ordered. "Push!"

I bore down. I let out a lot of strangled words that probably weren't words at all as my muscles and my body strained to accommodate the human beings that were passing through me.

I had good drugs, but I could still feel the stretch and the cramping and the way my whole body seized up until I couldn't breathe.

The doctor yelled for me to push again. And again.

Finally, I felt a release of something big, and fluid. There were voices. And then I heard a baby cry.

The doctor said from behind me, "You're not quite done. One more. One more."

"Mathias." My voice was hoarse as I ignored the doctor. "How does he look?"

"Hmm. A little bit unfortunate, but he'll clean up good, I think."

I hissed at him. "You ass."

All he did was smile down at me and run his hands through my hair. "One more," he said.

How could he be so calm?

The doctor ordered me to push again. I didn't recall much of it. I was dizzy and crazy at that point, and what I really wanted to do was lie down and sleep for about a million years.

I felt another release of something big, and I knew it was done.

The doctor was exclaiming how well I'd done. Mathias was congratulating me, but all I could do was close my eyes and breathe out in relief.

The afterbirth came quickly.

When I finally got my wind back, my first question was, "Are they healthy? Are they all right?"

Mathias was still holding my hand. But he had stepped away a little and was looking at something I couldn't see.

Finally, he turned and said, "Gremlin number one is all cleaned up. Gremlin number two is getting taken care of. They are perfect."

"You're not calling them both Gremlin."

"You'll be ready in a few minutes and then you can hold them," he said.

A nurse was cleaning me up, wrapping me in large pads like diapers. But everything was good.

"Ready to turn over?" he asked.

I was more than ready to look at anything other than pillows and a wall. Hands helped me get situated.

Mathias plumped pillows behind my head.

I wrestled into place, closed then opened my eyes and the nurse was standing before me with two white-wrapped bundles. He handed one to me and one to Mathias.

I reached out and brought my new baby to my chest, looking down at his sweet, scrunched up face and swirls of fine baby hair. I couldn't help but immediately put my lips to his forehead in a *welcome to the world* kiss.

I looked up at Mathias, but he was not looking at me. His fixed gaze and slightly open mouth were all for the newborn in his arms. He leaned forward and rubbed his nose against the baby's cheek. Then he looked at me and sat on the side of the bed, tilting the child in his arms so I could see him.

The doctor stood at the foot of my bed.

"A cursory exam has shown one Alpha, one Omega. We've marked their bracelets so you can tell the difference."

"Thank you."

Mathias held the baby in his arms close to his chest, just as I was doing.

"This certainly is a gremlin," he said.

"Ah, did you hear that?" I said to the baby in my arms. "Your father is an idiot."

"All right, then," he replied softly. "Real names. From our list. I like Kyro best."

I smiled at him, a warmth shifting behind my eyes. "I like it. Welcome to your life, Kyro."

"Now you," Mathias said.

I looked down at the tiny guy in my arms. "I like Elijah."

"Agreed." Mathias's eyes half-closed, glistening with emotion, as he spoke softly to the babe in my arms. "Welcome to the world, Elijah."

Neither of us had glanced once at their bracelets. We didn't care which one was Alpha, or which was Omega. These would be their names for now, and then they would become the people they wanted to be with help from their loving fathers. That was what we would do for them. And for Tybor and Luke as well.

I realized I had closed my eyes and was dozing. Later, I felt Mathias take the baby from me.

When I woke, it was to a most beautiful sight.

Mathias sat in the chair next to my bed, head down, eyes closed. He had one of our babies against his chest. He'd opened his shirt so the baby could be closer to his skin.

Through our bond I felt his resting state as if it were my own, his new-found tenderness, and his love.

In the past months, I had observed Mathias discovering a piece of himself he'd been missing his whole life. The home we'd both wished for when we were young, I on a chattel farm and he in his father's cold clutches, had now become something we could give each other.

It was the greatest of gifts.

THE END

Contact links for Wendy Rathbone:

Join my Facebook group Wendyland. I post updates, cover reveals, snippets, sales and other fun stuff every day:
https://www.facebook.com/groups/718074255203918/

Friend me on Facebook:
https://www.facebook.com/wendy.rathbone.3

Follow my Amazon author page:
https://www.amazon.com/Wendy-Rathbone/e/B00B0O9BMS/ref=dp_byline_cont_ebooks_1

Follow me on Bookbub:
https://www.bookbub.com/authors/wendy-rathbone

Dear Reader:

Thank you for reading *Single Omega Dad: The Omega Misfits Book 4.*

I loved writing an actual mpreg birth for the first time. With my background writing sci fi and alien biology, it was a perfect fit in my mind.

Next on my agenda is book 5 in *The Omega Misfits* series. I do not yet have a title, but you can expect many more books in this universe about misfit Omegas, Alpha Burns, and the romances that result. I hope you continue to stay along with me on this journey where I continue my discovery of this wonderful genre.

Happy Reading!

Love,
Wendy Rathbone

About Wendy Rathbone

Read Wendy Rathbone... where imposters and outcasts, princes and lost boys always find their happily every after.

I have written in all genres: sci-fi, fantasy, horror, paranormal, contemporary, erotica, romance. But I keep coming back to romance as the main focus. Gay romance. Male/male romance. The idea of two men falling in love is irresistible to me. It's all I write now.

All my books are available on Amazon and most are in Kindle Unlimited. So if you have the urge, go take a look. See what's on the shelf.

Male/male romance books by Wendy:

The Kingdom of Slaves Series (contemporary fantasy mm romance)

The Slave Palace
The Slave Harem
Master of Halloween (short story)

The Omega Misfits (Omegaverse mm romance)

Trust No Alpha
The Alpha's Fake Mate
Alpha's Embrace
Single Omega Dad

The Imposter Series (fantasy mm romance)

The Imposter Prince
The Imposter King

The Moonling Prince Series (fantasy, sci fi mm romance)

The Moonling Prince
The Coming of the Light

The Foundling Series (contemporary billionaire mm romance trilogy)

Rescue Me
Sacrifice Me
Remember Me

The Fantastic Immortals Series (fantasy/myth mm romance)

Ganymede: Abducted by the Gods
Zeus: Conquering his Heart

Stand Alone Novels

Sci Fi MM Romance

Solstice Gift (holiday)
Not Another Hero
Cocky Virgin Prince
Prey
Scoundrel
The Android and the Thief (Second edition coming May 2020)
Letters to an Android

Fantasy MM Romance

Lord Vampyre
Lace
Snow of the White Hills (mm fairy tale)
The Elves of Christmas (holiday fantasy mm romance)

Contemporary MM Romance

Romantically Incorrect
Snowfall and Romance (Christmas novel)
The Bodyguard's Valentine
Buying You

Alpha's Embrace
(The Omega Misfits #3)
Wendy Rathbone

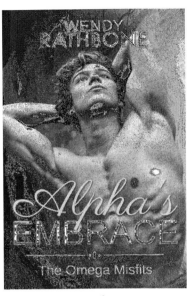

I am Misha.

My name was given to me at birth by the doctor who delivered me. I have never known my parents. I live in a ten by ten space with one window, a sink and toilet, a bed and a locked door. Once a day I'm taken to an outdoor exercise area. I am allowed a limited access tablet and tutored online by computer programs. I have one friend I talk to through a tiny crack in the wall. His name is Cedric and he has trouble keeping himself quiet. When he isn't talking to me about monsters and demons, he screams all the time.

Why is my life so isolated and depressing? Because I am a Sylph. Sylphs are the byproduct of illegal Omega to Omega matings. We are all beautiful, but 99.9% are born insane. The rarest of Sylphs, like me, show no outward signs of madness or brain damage, but we live in institutions because we cannot be trusted.

All of us Sylphs who have lived long enough to pass through puberty have hypersexual disorder which makes life even more difficult for us, let alone our keepers. It is like something Alphas call the Burn, a mating urge Alphas experience once every couple of months.

But we're Sylphs, not Alphas, and this Burn thing? We experience it all the time. It's a huge problem and why we are kept isolated. Most of us don't survive through our teens because of it.

One day, a handsome Alpha comes to interview and study me. He calls himself the Chief of Staff but his real name is Geo. Like magic, I fall in love with him instantly. I do everything I can to seduce him. He will have none of it because touch between an Alpha and a Sylph is taboo. But I have plans. No matter what, I intend to bond him and make him mine. Forever.

A non-shifter Alpha/Omega-Sylph love story of forbidden love, rescue, and HEA. Standalone read. No Mpreg. 58k words.

222

TRUST NO ALPHA
The Omega Misfits, Book 1
Wendy Rathbone

It's a world gone mad. The Alphas are out of control. When you discover you're not who you thought you were, the nightmare begins.

KRIS
At age eighteen, life as he knows it is over for Kris. A secret to his nature he was not aware of has been revealed.

Now, kept as a prisoner in a locked room in the mansion of his wealthy father, Kris is at the mercy of Alpha laws and Alpha domination.

Things take a turn for the worse when his own litter mate threatens him, and his father starts behaving strangely around him.

Escape is his only hope. But where can he go in a world that allows him no rights?

THORNE
Marked as a dangerous Alpha, and living a secluded life alone and unloved, Thorne still grieves for the mate whose death he feels responsible for.

Years have passed, and he refuses to even try to function in normal society.

One day he discovers a young man on his property, disheveled, desperate, and scared. He acts like a runaway Omega, but he doesn't smell like one.

What is this boy? And why does Thorne feel an immediate need to protect him? To bond him? To make him his?

A non-shifter, Omegaverse love story of rescue, first time, fertility issues and an HEA. Standalone read. 65,500 words. (While Omegas are birth-fathers in this universe, there is no on-page mpreg in this book.)

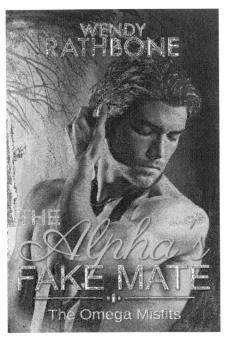

THE ALPHA'S FAKE MATE
The Omega Misfits, Book 2
Wendy Rathbone

The Alphas think they own everything. Including people. Well, I'm here to say they don't own me, and I will never let one of those bastards touch me again.

The frenzy of their Burn cannot be trusted. I know from experience. My first time with an Alpha nearly ended in my death. And because of the laws which favor Alpha rights, and place a large number of unbonded, adult Omegas on chattel farms, my abuser can never be tried for his crimes against me.

Omegas are being hurt. Omegas are dying.

All Alphas are violent. Or so I believe. Until I meet Orion.

Ori is everything a guy could want in a mate. Six foot three. Beautiful brown wavy hair. Bright, dark eyes. Muscles like chiseled marble. He even says "please" and "thank you" at all the right times. He's got it all, except he's an Alpha.

Though he has given me a room in his home free of charge, and has signed fake paperwork saying we are bonded so I don't have to answer my attacker's claim, can I trust him?

But now I'm in danger. If I don't take a real mate, my life as I know it will be over. Can I believe in the goodness of Ori? Can I learn to love again?

A non-shifter, fake mate, Alpha/Omega love story. Rescue. First time. Omegaverse. Mpreg. Healing from sexual trauma. (All books in The Omega Misfits series are standalone reads and can be read in any order.) 61k words.

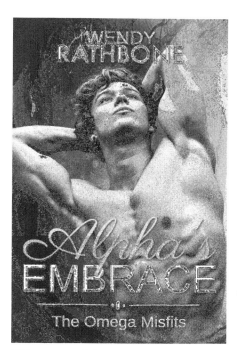

ALPHA'S EMBRACE
The Omega Misfits, Book 3
Wendy Rathbone

I am Misha. My name was given to me at birth by the doctor who delivered me. I have never known my parents. I live in a ten by ten space with one window, a sink and toilet, a bed and a locked door. Once a day I'm taken to an outdoor exercise area. I am allowed a limited access tablet and tutored online by computer programs. I have one friend I talk to through a tiny crack in the wall. His name is Cedric and he has trouble keeping himself quiet. When he isn't talking to me about monsters and demons, he screams all the time.

Why is my life so isolated and depressing? Because I am a Sylph. Sylphs are the byproduct of illegal Omega to Omega matings. We are all beautiful, but 99.9% are born insane. The rarest of Sylphs, like me, show no outward signs of madness or brain damage, but we live in institutions because we cannot be trusted.

All of us Sylphs who have lived long enough to pass through puberty have hypersexual disorder which makes life even more difficult for us, let alone our keepers. It is like something Alphas call the Burn, a mating urge Alphas experience once every couple of months.

But we're Sylphs, not Alphas, and this Burn thing? We experience it all the time. It's a huge problem and why we are kept isolated. Most of us don't survive through our teens because of it.

One day, a handsome Alpha comes to interview and study me. He calls himself the Chief of Staff but his real name is Geo. Like magic, I fall in love with him instantly. I do everything I can to seduce him. He will have none of it because touch between an Alpha and a Sylph is taboo. But I have plans. No matter what, I intend to bond him and make him mine. Forever.

A non-shifter Alpha/Omega-Sylph love story of forbidden love, rescue, and HEA. Standalone read. No Mpreg. 58k words.

THE SLAVE HAREM
Wendy Rathbone

The slave harem is all. If you enter, you can never leave. Contact with the outside world is forbidden.

With a secret talent for seeing auras of physical and emotional arousal, Ren, a sought-after pleasure slave, is sold to a mysterious master in a foreign land where he will become part of a collection of beautiful men.

Though the men appear welcoming, there is competition and jealousy among the ranks. And their mysterious master who is heard but never seen elicits more questions than answers.

One friendly slave, Li Po, helps Ren settle in, but it is the voiceless man, Zanti, who draws Ren's attention. With his wicked beauty and bratty scowls, Zanti is the least welcoming of them all, and Ren's training and control are put to the test.

Gay harem, slow-burn, enemies to lovers. Extraordinary and strange. Hot and cold. This book explores the many levels of sex, lust, loneliness and belonging. And maybe, just maybe, there can be love.

THE SLAVE PALACE
Wulf and Locke
WENDY RATHBONE

Conquered. Captured. Sold as a pleasure slave.

After being taken as a prisoner of war, Wulf fights his captors and is sold as a One-Night Thrall to be used and abused, then put to death. He is purchased by a high ranking master of the famous Slave Palace. Why Locke buys him, Wulf has no clue, but something about this master is intriguing. Instead of abuse, Wulf is plied with luxuries he has never known by a man who actually seems to respect him.

Jaded. Looking for a challenge.

Eminent Master Locke takes on a bet with his best friend that he can't train and tame a dangerous One-Night Thrall in ten days. But something about this slave stirs him like no other before. All bets aside, Locke has the urge to keep Wulf, as well as save his life. But Wulf is fierce, unwilling, and his consent papers have been forged. If Wulf doesn't soon submit to his role as a slave, he will be sent to death as a prisoner of war.

A sweet, slow-burn love story taking place on an alternate contemporary Earth where owning pleasure slaves is legal.

LORD VAMPYRE
Wendy Rathbone

When Lord Neverelle becomes a guest at Cliffside Keep, Vanni watches helplessly as Damion, the young man he's grown up with and secretly loves, falls for the alluring and seductive stranger. Lord Neverelle is danger incarnate, and soon takes control of the household.

Not satisfied with Damion alone, Never uses a vampire trick called "the tempt" to compel Vanni, who is swept into a love triangle that includes fiery passion and nightly threesomes.

Now Vanni must ask himself, is any of this consensual? And what about Damion—does he really want to be with Vanni, or is it all a sensual play controlled by vampire compulsion?

M/M and M/M/M romance.

The Imposter Prince
Book 1 in The Imposter Series
Wendy Rathbone

His love for an enemy prince threatens his very life.

Dare does not mind serving the spoiled and cruel Prince Darius. Growing up with him, Dare does everything for Darius including homework, bed play demands, and even doubling for him as the prince grows too paranoid to face even the smallest of crowds.

But everything changes in a single moment when Dare, while posing as Darius, is abducted by the enemy.

A captive in a new and hostile land, Dare meets another prince who seems just as indulged and rotten as Darius— until Dare gets to know him, until they fall in love. Against his will, Dare must continue to play the role of Prince Darius for real, or risk everything: his love, his land, and his very life.

His only chance for survival is to keep a secret from the one he loves, a secret that is also killing him.

A male/male, enemies to lovers novel of mad kings, troubled princes, abduction, fevers, cold dungeons, warm hearths, comfort, wine, and true love.

BUYING YOU
Wendy Rathbone

It's one thing to be a beautiful cover model on billboards, buses and magazine covers. It's quite another to be sold as one.

Prized for his looks, Dane knows it's shallow, but he is on his way to having it all. It feels good to be gorgeous, smart and have top designers from around the world requesting him.

When he returns to his hometown to participate in a small Date-For-Charity auction, it seems harmless enough—until a hooded man walks in and bids higher on him than anyone else. Dane is intrigued but nervous when he finds out the guy has vanished after the winning bid, leaving only a limo behind to whisk Dane off into the night.

Enemies to lovers, opposites attract, and hot steamy nights that challenge two guys' trust issues along with their biggest fears.

SONS OF NEVERLAND
A Deliciously Dark Male/Male Romance
Della Van Hise

Set against a backdrop of contemporary culture, *Sons of Neverland* explores the universal questions of love, sex and death - the three most crucial challenges every human being must face. Stefan London is a grieving man, suffering through the loss of his young daughter. When he goes to a science fiction convention in the hopes of meeting her friends, he encounters instead a man who is dangerously seductive. Lured into the night, Stefan soon discovers himself in a world where vampires are real, and immortality is only a kiss away.

But the price of eternal life is high, and as his handsome maker warns, "Through my blood you will learn a secret that will compel you to live forever, yet a secret so sinister it will haunt you for that same eternity."

The secret will haunt you, too.

A deliciously dark male/male romance. First time, enemies to lovers, love/hate relationship, HEA.

YEAR OF THE RAM
Della Van Hise

Year of the Ram was described by one reviewer as... "A space-faring gay romance full of love, angst, and longing."

Only after Star Commander Morgan Diego becomes an exile as a result of a Galaxy Corps political blunder does he begin to realize how much he valued the companionship of his second in command - the mysterious Lucien, an Alfarian who is more elfen than human, with peculiar powers & abilities which begin to unfold as he, too, realizes what he has lost.

Separated by circumstance from his former life, Morgan is thrust into a world where he must survive by his wits. When he meets a peculiar little old man calling himself Kim Le, Morgan finds himself in a situation where he is required to master The Art - not only a form of human & extraterrestrial martial arts, but a way of living that will alter his life forever.

At the temple, he is introduced to his new teacher, another Alfarian man who begins to steal his heart - a heart which is already promised to Lucien. Torn and conflicted, Morgan struggles with the world he left behind and the world he now inhabits.

Beginning to believe he may never again return to his ship and to the friends and loved ones he left behind, he is all the more frustrated and heartbroken when a new Master arrives at the temple: a man to whom Morgan is immediately drawn both mentally and physically, a man who is strikingly familiar... yet utterly alien.

Eye Scry Publications
www.eyescrypublications.com

Made in the USA
Middletown, DE
15 January 2023

22210464R00139